Frederick Germaine
Presents

As We Lay
A   True   Love Novel

Also by Frederick Germaine
Ladies' Man: An Entertaining Love Novel
Eye Candy: A Romantic Love Novel
Lovers: An Exciting Love Novel
Ladies' Man 2: An Entertaining Love Novel

Copyright © 2016 by Frederick Germaine
Published by: F. Germaine Publishing
Cover Layout & Design: Brand Concepts Creative Media
Photography: Reggie Anderson
Models: Shalonda Shay Anderson & Tresha Lettsome
ISBN: 978-0-692-71944-2

Printed in the United States of America.

Dedication:

To everyone laying with the wrong person. You better be careful!

AS WE LAY

A TRUE LOVE NOVEL

F. GERMAINE PUBLISHING
ATLANTA, GEORGIA

WWW.FREDERICKGERMAINE.COM

PROLOGUE
SHOTS FIRED

"Yeah, that's right you low down son-of-a-bitch wake up," said the familiar female voice into my ear. Then she slapped my face a couple of times. "Seems like that gas agent I gave you is finally wearing off. And just in time so you can witness your own death."

"Where am I?" I asked opening my eyes. My vision was blurred as I attempted to look around.

"Somewhere isolated for what I need to do with you," she responded.

From what I could make out, we had to be in a basement or cellar. The area was dark and cold. The only thing illuminating the room were bright glowing lights throughout the floor. Since I still couldn't see fully, I assumed they were candles.

There were no clothes on me except for a pair of boxers. I couldn't move because the back of my body was confined to a large iron pole. The pole had to support the foundation of the building because there were identical ones throughout the room. My hands were above my head with my fingers interlocked. They were tied with twine to the pole and I couldn't move them at all. Below, my ankles were crossed and tightly tied as well.

"What kind of contraption is this?" I asked aimlessly still trying to see.

"Don't worry, its secure enough to keep you where I want you," she replied. "I should cut your handsome face up so you can feel how much pain you caused me."

She pressed a cold object onto my forehead and slowly began to move downwards. I could tell it was a knife and a long one at that. It was the non-sharpen end that was moving downwards. By the time the knife reached my jawline, she turned the blade over and cut a gash near my chin.

"Ah, damn you!" I shouted out.

"What's the matter, Stewart, you like dishing out pain but can't take it?" Drops of blood began to fall onto my chest as she continued to move the blade down my body. "Let's see, maybe I should cut your heart out and give you mine. No, that won't work because mine is all broken. I think I should damage something that means more to you."

"What the hell are you doing?" I asked as the knife was at my boxer's waistline.

"I'm going to cut your dick off," she said and laughed. "Then while you bleed to death, I'm going to shove it into your mouth so you can't scream anymore."

She was dead serious and I knew it. I tried to wiggle free but my hands and feet were tied too tight. With the flick of her wrist, she cut my underwear off as they fell to the floor. I swallowed a gulp as I couldn't believe what was happening.

Before she could execute her plan, the door in front of us was kicked open. A tunnel of cold air rushed in and onto my body. Goosebumps quickly formed on me as the many of the once-lit candles had all blown out. There was a person who stood by the door.

"What are you doing here? You're not supposed to know about this."

"Put the knife down and let him go."

"I'm not putting this knife down for you, him, or anyone else."

"I swear I'll shoot if you don't put the knife down."

"No!"

"I'm going to shoot on the count of three if you don't drop that knife."

"Go ahead, I dare you."

"Don't you make me do this! One, two..."

PART I

AN EXTRAORDINARY MAN

SIX MONTHS EARLIER

CHAPTER 1

"Girl, where are you?"

"I'm trying to find a parking space. Are you there already?"

"Yes, Ashley, I'm standing right here at the front door of Octane Coffee Bar. I can't believe you're late."

"Jennifer, don't blame me it's the Atlanta traffic as always."

"Well, I'm going inside now. I'll order us something to drink and grab a seat as well."

"Okay, I'll see you in a bit."

Jennifer hung up her cell phone and stuffed it into her small purse. As she began to reach for the front door of the establishment, a stranger suddenly interrupted her.

"Let me get that for you," said a tall man opening the door for her. "Someone as gorgeous as you should always have a man opening doors for you."

"Thank you," she said with a sly grin. Then she entered into the building.

"Hey, by the way, I'm Randle."

"Nice meeting you, Randle."

Jennifer calmly turned around and rolled her eyes once Randle was out of her view. With a brisk stride, she made her way to the front counter to place an order. Randle was right on her heels like a lost puppy dog or better yet a dog in heat. He was checking out her posterior as she had plenty to offer.

"I'm sorry, I didn't get your name."

"I didn't give it to you, Randle," she said turning her head back momentarily. Then she continued onwards.

"Maybe this would be a good time for us to get to know each other," he said eagerly. "I would love for you to join me for a cup of coffee."

The pair had now made it to the front counter and Jennifer was somewhat annoyed by her new found friend. She turned to him once again.

"Sorry, Randle, I'm actually meeting someone here. And besides, I really don't have the time to meet new people."

Dejected, Randle calmly nodded his head as if he understood. Jennifer then placed her order. She grabbed some cash out of her purse and handed it to the clerk in front of her. After which, she received her order. Before she could depart, Randle decided to speak again.

"You know I try to be nice to you bougie stuck up women," he said with anger in his voice. "But some of y'all just don't crack."

Jennifer slightly hesitated but looked him up and down. Without saying a word, she rolled her eyes right in front of him. The clerk, who was witnessing this, decided to intervene before an argument ensued.

"Sir, are you ready to order?" the clerk asked as Jennifer walked away.

"Yeah, I guess I am," he answered turning his back away from Jennifer's departure.

"Well, what would you like, sir?"

"Just give me whatever she had."

Without giving the man a second thought, Jennifer continued to stroll throughout the coffee shop looking for a place to sit. With beverages in tow, she finally found a cozy table with two chairs near the huge front window. There she took a seat and briefly admired people walking on the sidewalk while a policeman was directing traffic in the street. Meanwhile, inside the place was buzzing with people having conversations and everyone else glued to their laptops. While she waited, Jennifer put the cup of beverage to her lips.

"There you are," said Ashley walking up to Jennifer's table. "I've been strolling around here for at least a minute trying to find you. I should have known to look near the window."

"Girl, it's about time you got here," said Jennifer placing her cup back on the table. "Come on take a seat so we can chat."

Finally, the two thirty-something women were face-to-face anticipating the conversation that was about to take place. Both of them were eager to hear what the other one had to say.

Jennifer, a successful professional, worked in real estate for the last ten years. Miraculously, she found a way to survive through the housing crash. And now that the market had turned for the better, she was her own real estate broker. It was small operation but at least it belonged to her. By now, you probably guessed she was confident, never bashful, spoke her mind, and, most importantly, very attractive.

Ashley, on the other hand, was the complete opposite. Although she didn't have the entrepreneur spirit as Jennifer, she did work in administration at the corporate level for an energy company. She was quiet, reserved, and it took a lot to get her riled up. In a crowd, she could turn a few heads but not as many as her sister Jennifer could.

Unlike many counterparts, these two were not transplants to the city. They were born and raised in Atlanta with Jennifer being two years older than Ashley. Both attended college outside the state of Georgia and after graduation settled back into Atlanta.

"So what did you get me?" Ashley asked as she sat down looking at the cup in front of her.

"It's your favorite," Jennifer replied. Then she slightly pushed the cup towards her sister.

"Super regular, huh?"

"Of course because you won't settle for anything else."

Ashley quickly took a small sip from the cup and then another. Then she placed the beverage back on the table in front of her.

"Okay, Jennifer, spill the beans because I don't have a lot of time. You know my boss gets anal if I return from my lunch break a few minutes late."

"How do you deal with working for someone like that? You should really consider starting your own business and becoming an employer instead of an employee."

"It's really not that bad. Yes, I have to deal with a few people I don't care for but overall it's a good company. The pay and benefits are good and besides everyone is not cut out to be a boss like you."

"Well, I guess you're right, Ashley."

"Um, let's get to the reason why you brought me here," Ashley announced. Then she pointed at her watch. "Time is of the essence."

"You're going to love to hear how he and I met," Jennifer proclaimed with a bright smile. "Plus, he's an extraordinary man."

"Oh my God, please don't tell me how he claims to be a prince of small foreign country. Or better yet, how he plans to buy you the world in a blink of an eye."

"You can cut the sarcasm, Ashley. It's been quite a while since I fell for a man who told me those lies."

"Thank goodness. I was beginning to think I was wasting my time hearing another fairy tale."

"Are you done having fun now?"

"Okay, I promise not to say another word."

"That's good. Now sit there and relax while I tell

you the story."

Ashley did as her older sister requested. She listened emphatically and was intrigued. She wanted to know what was so different about this new guy. But more importantly, she wanted to know why Jennifer claimed he was so extraordinary.

CHAPTER 2

There I was sitting impatiently in the large, yet plush, service lounge at the dealership waiting for my car. It was quite busy for a Monday morning but that was expected. To my left, I noticed a woman waiting just like me. Instead of checking out the scenery, she had her eyes glued to the tablet she was holding. I assumed it had to be the latest social media gossip because she never seemed to look up. Near her was a gentleman casually flipping through a magazine. Other customers were watching the large flat screen while sipping on their morning fix of coffee. I looked at my watch again and it was nine forty-five. Then I shook my head wondering what was taking so long.

"Ah, there you are, Mr. Sellers," said a young man

approaching me from the right. It was Josh my service advisor.

"So am I all set to go?" I asked while standing up.

"Not exactly, sir. It seems like I'm the bearer of bad news this morning."

"What seems to be the problem, Josh?"

"Well, the technician noticed your front rotors need to be replaced in addition to changing out your brake pads."

"Okay, then have him replace the rotors so I can be on my way."

"That's where the problem exist, sir. Unfortunately, we don't have the rotors in stock for your S-class. I've went ahead and ordered the parts through our warehouse and a courier should have them here in thirty minutes."

"Jeesh!"

"I know, sir. I'm sorry for the inconvenience."

"I was expecting to be out of here by now," I said looking at my watch again. "I guess I'll have to wait it out."

"Actually, sir, I can put you in a loaner vehicle if that would help."

"No, don't worry about it, Josh. I'll just wait."

"As soon as the parts arrive, we'll get you all taken care of. Plus, I'll make sure the guys in detail wash your car."

"Okay, that's fine."

Josh gave me a firm handshake as to solidify everything was going to work out alright. As he walked away, I sat back down in the comfy leather chair. As I did, I noticed the woman to my left quickly looking away from me. Apparently, Ms. Nosey found our conversation more consuming than her tablet. I simply chuckled and smile. Then I retrieved my cell phone from my pocket.

One of the perks of working for a major insurance company, as an account manager, was flexibility and having my own secretary. At times like these, my secretary would often reschedule appointments, confirm important meetings, and allow me not to forget anything in between. She was the one person I needed to speak with this morning. Therefore, I promptly dialed her number and placed the cell phone to my ear. While I waited for her to answer, I cleared my throat.

"Good morning, this is Lauren," said the innocent sounding voice on the other end. "How can I assist you?"

"Good morning, Lauren, it's me," I answered in my normal tone.

"Oh, hello, Mr. Sellers. I noticed you're not in your office right now. Is everything okay?"

"Yes, everything is fine. I'm actually at my car

dealership having some minor work performed. Unfortunately, it is taking longer than I had anticipated."

"Do you need me to come and pick you up?"

"No, that's not necessary, Lauren. I should be out of here shortly."

"Is there anything you need for me to do in the interim until you get here?"

"Well, first things first."

"Okay, I just grabbed my pen so I won't miss anything important while I listen."

"Lauren, how long have you been working for our company now as a temp?"

"Mr. Sellers, today marks the beginning of my third week."

"Now, do you remember the first day you reported to work?"

"Yes I do."

"Remember how I told you to simply address me as 'Stewart' like everyone else."

"Yes."

"Well, I actually mean that, Lauren. You don't have to be so formal with me. Everyone in the office blends in like one big happy family."

"I'm sorry, Mr. Sellers. It's just that the temp

company, who assigned me here, suggested it."

"Don't worry, Lauren, I promise no one is going to reprimand you. Please, from now on just address me as Stewart."

"Yes, sir, Mr. Sellers. Um, I mean, Stewart."

"Alright, now that we're on the same page, let me know what's on the calendar for today."

Lauren put down the pen she was holding and turned to the computer on her desk. I could hear her fingers typing away on the keyboard. In a matter of seconds, she had my daily calendar in front of her.

"For starters, you have a one o'clock meeting with one of your accounts. It's the Luxemburg Group account."

"Yeah, they weren't too excited about their loss run report last quarter or how we handled some of their liability claims. They want to meet, with me, on how to limit their future exposure. I'm not too thrilled about delivering bad news to them today."

"You should lighten the load by offering your client something to eat during the meeting?"

"What did you have in mind, Lauren?"

"Specialty pastries served with hot or cold beverages should do the trick."

"Yes, that sounds tasty. Go ahead and put in the

order but make sure they deliver on time."

"I'm on it."

"What else do I have going on today?"

"You have a mandatory department meeting at three. Then a follow up call to a potential client at four."

"Okay, that doesn't seem like nothing too hectic. If you need to reach me just dial my cell phone."

"Sure thing, Stewart. I'll see you when you get here."

After I ended my conversation with Lauren, I strolled through the dealership showroom floor browsing at the latest models. Then I sat back down and flipped through a magazine like the gentleman I noticed earlier.

Right before noon, Josh notified me my car was fully serviced and I could be on my way. When I retrieved my car, it was clean inside and out just like he promised. I pressed on the accelerator and headed for the office. I was anxious to see what pastries Lauren had ordered. I definitely needed a sugar rush to give me a boost for the day.

CHAPTER 3

"For heaven's sake, where have you been?" Daniel asked his colleague as she exited the women's restroom. He had a stack of paperwork in his hand and stopped momentarily. "And besides that, you look awful. Are you okay?"

"I just got back from my lunch break about five minutes ago," Ashley replied. She stood in the isle, next to him, with her head slightly tilted down. "I really don't feel that well."

Daniel and Ashley worked in the same department as their desk were in close proximity to each other. He was married for almost a year now and always chatted about it. They both reported to Charlene, their supervisor, who had a mean streak in her.

"What did you eat for lunch?"

"All I had was a cup of coffee from Octane Coffee Bar."

"Ashley, you can't just drink coffee all day without eating and not putting something on your stomach."

"I know, Daniel, you mentioned that to me before. I'd better head to my desk and get some aspirin."

"Wait, I don't think you want to go there right now."

"Why?"

"Charlene came by looking for you a few seconds ago."

"What did she want now?"

"She just asked if you had returned back from lunch."

"Well, what did you tell her?"

"I told her I saw you headed for the mailroom not too long ago."

"Thanks for covering for me, Daniel."

"Hey, it's no problem. Now grab a few of these documents and follow me to the copier room. I think I can find some aspirin along the way."

"Okay, lead the way."

Ashley took half of Daniel's paperwork and the pair

made their way to the copier room which was filled with many machines. It was on the same floor but on the other side of the building. Along the way, he was able to retrieve some aspirin from a coworker. As the two entered the room, they noticed someone else making copies also. They made their way to another machine to ensure some privacy.

"I'll work on this stack I have," he said. "And you can work on what you have."

"Yeah, it shouldn't take us that long," she said.

"After this, I have to head back to my desk and make a few phone calls or my wife is going to kill me."

"Kill you for what, Daniel?"

"We decided to move out of our apartment and buy a house. I promised her I would contact a few real estate agents today."

"I don't think she'll go that far if you didn't make a few phone calls."

"Ashley, you don't know my wife, Terri, like I do. And besides, she's super anxious since we have a new addition coming."

"Are you saying what I think you're saying, Daniel?"

"You betcha."

"Well congratulations," she exclaimed pausing for a

moment with a smile. "How far along is she?"

"Only six weeks now," he said proudly as he stop feeding the copy machine. "But nine months will be here before we know it."

"Come to think about it, you may only have to make one phone call."

"Why do you say that?"

"My sister is a top-producing real estate broker right here in Atlanta."

"Oh really."

"Yes, she has her own realty company as well. I'm sure she could negotiate a great deal for you. I'd love to refer you to her."

"I'm sold, Ashley."

"So what area would you and your wife like to buy a house in?"

"We're seriously thinking about Kennesaw."

"That's a bit further out but it's a nice scenic area."

"Yeah, but it fits who we are."

As they both continued their conversation, in walks Charlene. She seemed a bit frustrated and was breathing heavily. The other person, in the room, looked up briefly then went back to copying his documents.

"There you are," said Charlene looking at Ashley.

"I thought I might find you in here."

"Yes, I had to stop by the copier room after I left the mailroom," said Ashley in a serious tone. Meanwhile, Daniel said nothing and continued to look busy.

"I must have just missed you. I hate that I walked down and back up those flights of stairs."

"Sorry you missed me, Charlene. I took the elevator and that's probably why."

"Well, at least I got my daily cardio regimen in. Anyway, when you're done in here come straight to my office."

"I'll be done in here shortly and will be on my way."

Charlene simply nodded giving her approval. Then she turned around and slipped out the copier room as quickly as she entered. Ashley worked a little bit faster wondering what Charlene wanted now. Meanwhile, Daniel was excited that he only had to make one phone call.

CHAPTER 4

It was right around eleven o'clock in the morning when I departed from my condo in Druid Hills. On this particular Saturday, I had my usual set of tasks to take care of. First, on the agenda, was my visit to my barbershop for a precision haircut. Afterwards, I would get my car washed and detailed. Lastly, I would make a quick trip to the cleaners and grocery store. Even though it seemed like not much to do, those simple tasks almost always consumed my entire day.

The weather couldn't have been any better for a clear sunny summer day. It had to be at least eighty-five degrees already but I really didn't care. I had the air condition on ice cold in my S-class while grooving to some mellow jazz tunes. Instead of taking the interstate, I decided to take the scenic route by using the back surface roads to Decatur. That's where the barbershop I had been using for a long time now was located.

Within the next twenty minutes, I had pulled up to Walter's Barbershop. Coincidentally, Walter was my barber and the owner of the business. He was an older gentleman who dressed nice. His attire usually consisted of slacks, a pressed shirt, and comfortable shoes for standing. The white barber coat he wore was always white as snow, cleaned, and pressed. He was partially bald on the top of his head. Any remaining hair on the side and back of his head was grey. After working nearly all his life on the railroads, he retired with a handsome savings and pension. To avoid being bored all day, or listening to his wife fuss, he decided to open a barbershop which was his passion.

"Hi Walter," I said entering the establishment. He was standing near his chair located by the front door.

"Hey there, Stewart," he said cleaning his chair with a hair duster. "You're just in time for your appointment. Come on and take a seat."

"So I see you are packed as usual," I said looking around. I noticed all the barbers had clients in their chair. Plus, there had to be at least fifteen people waiting. "I'm glad I called ahead and scheduled an appointment."

"Yeah, it always helps to have one," he said putting a black cape over me. "And besides, I like to service my loyal customers like yourself. I believe you've been coming here for about five years now."

"More like ten, Walter."

"Has it really been that long?"

"Yes it has."

Walter placed a white neck strip on me and then tightened up the cape. He grabbed a comb from an array of barber utensils situated behind the chair. Then he maneuvered it throughout my hair and walked in front of me.

"Okay, so how do you want it today?"

"The same as usual, Walter. Low fade on the sides and just cut off the wild hairs all the way around."

"You got it, Stewart."

After I gave the instructions, he moved behind my chair and retrieved a pair of silver clippers. With careful precision and personal technique, he began to work his magic.

"How's everything at the job going?" he asked.

"Just fine," I replied. "I have no complaints.

"I guess there's always someone in need for insurance especially when you're selling it."

"Well, actually, Walter I don't sell insurance. I'm an account manager for an insurance company. I'm the middleman between my clients and the insurance company."

"That's right Stewart, I keep confusing you with an insurance agent," he said pausing for a moment. Then he looked down at my left hand. "I see you're still not wearing a wedding band."

"No, I haven't made it that far, Walter," I said laughing a little. "Believe it or not, I'm still an eligible bachelor."

"What are you waiting for?"

"I just haven't found that special person I guess."

"I figure you to be somewhere in your early thirties, right?"

"I'm actually thirty-five."

"You know when I was your age, my wife and I had already been married for fifteen years."

"No disrespect Walter but that was a long time ago. Things are so much different now."

"Yeah, but back in my day a man would have to court a woman. It was called courting."

"Courting?"

"You never heard of that word before, Stewart?"

"I have but it's been a while since I heard someone use that word."

"Don't let that forgotten word fool you, youngster. Courting was something magnificent back in my day."

"How so?"

"Well, a man showered only one woman with love, loyalty, and respect. He did it as a form of commitment hoping one day she would be his wife."

"Go ahead, I'm listening."

"And the woman reciprocated her love back to him as well. Because every woman wants to be that man's only woman he's showing interest to."

"Let me guess, Walter, there wasn't any pre-marital sex, huh?"

"No, there wasn't a lot of that going on. Why would there need to be?"

"Come on, Walter, you know every man has his needs."

By now, Walter had positioned himself in front of me. He was still cutting my hair but paused again for a moment to look at me. As he did, I slightly looked up at him.

"You remember Christmas when you were a kid, right?"

"Yeah, I sure do."

"Now remember the best Christmas ever when you wanted something so bad and waited all year for Santa to bring it to you."

"It was a BMX bike I had my eye on forever. I did everything right the whole year hoping I would get it."

"Do you remember Christmas morning seeing your BMX bike in the living room next to the tree?" he asked.

"Man, do I!" I replied with excitement as if I was a kid again.

"Well, how did it feel?"

"It was the best feeling in the world."

"That's my point I'm driving home to you, Stewart, about courting and no pre-marital sex back in my day."

"Okay, you got me. I see what you're saying."

"Truth be told, the night my wife and I consummated our marriage it had to be the best feeling in the world for me as well."

Walter and I continued our dialogue as he finished up my haircut. Afterwards, he added some hot shaving cream to my face and shaved me with a straight razor. When everything was complete, I paid him and left a generous tip. Then we shook hands as I anticipated seeing him again in a few weeks.

As I departed the barbershop, in my car, I thought about what Walter and I just talked about. In particular, how he spoke about 'courting' back in his day. I kind of chuckled a bit to myself and never gave it a second thought again. Quickly, I maneuvered into traffic as I had other tasks to complete.

CHAPTER 5

"Dammit, Jennifer, how in the hell can you just cut me off all of a sudden? Keith asked his former lover, yelling through his cell phone.

"It's not all of a sudden, Keith," replied Jennifer calmly through her cell phone as well. "As a matter of fact, I told you almost three weeks ago we were through."

"Didn't I treat you good, baby?"

"Yes, you did, Keith. But through it all, there was more bad than good."

"Shit, there you go complaining again! Don't you know how to appreciate a good man?"

"Keith, I know you can't be serious with that statement."

"The hell I'm not serious, woman," he stated.

"What about all the good things I did for you no one else did?"

"I can't even remember all that many good things you did for me," she added rolling her eyes.

"Baby, I surprised you with roses at your job," he said with empathy. "I took you on a weekend getaway to the Bahamas and even fixed your kitchen sink."

"Roses should be given to a women often, she said. "And as far as the trip to the Bahamas, you were trying to make up for when I caught you cheating. As for the kitchen sink, every man should be skilled with his hands."

"There you go again turning positive things, I did for you, around and putting me in the wrong."

"Keith, the truth is the truth. What about the woman who showed up at my office claiming she wanted to look at real estate?"

"Um, what woman, Jennifer?"

"Oh, now look who has amnesia. The damn woman you were cheating with, Keith!"

"Baby, you never really let me fully explain that situation to you."

"Don't worry she did."

"So I guess this is really it after a whole year, huh?"

"Yes, it's finally over between us. But I thank God

the nightmare only lasted for ten months."

"Fuck it," he said nearly yelling again. "I'm coming over there right now to get the rest of my clothes and shoes out of your closet."

"No the hell you're not!" she snapped. Keith could tell by her tone she was dead serious. "You must be a damn fool if you think I'm going to let you step a foot back in my home."

"Well, how the hell am I supposed to get the rest of my stuff?"

"I'll mail them to you."

"No, that's not going to work. Jennifer, you better come up with one better than that."

"Okay, Keith, I'll put your remaining things in a box and place it on the front porch."

"Woman, have you forgotten I have very expensive taste is clothes and shoes?"

"Trust me, no one is going to take your box off my porch. Come by in an hour when I'll be gone on my date by then."

"Did you say a date?"

"Yes, Keith, I did."

"So he must be the rebound guy, huh?"

"No, he's an extraordinary man. Even my sister,

Ashley, thinks so."

"You mean the same Ashley who couldn't get a man if I delivered myself to her all wrapped up with a pretty bow on top," he said laughing hysterically.

"Watch it, Keith," she said firing back.

"Just make sure the box is on the front porch when I get there," he said in a serious demeanor. "And when he hurts you more than I did, don't say I didn't warn you."

"When you pick up your box, don't you ever call me again," she said in a resounding tone. "And I mean it!"

Before Keith had a chance to respond, Jennifer had quickly disconnected the call. She stood there in her bedroom of her Alpharetta townhome visibly shaken. Starring at her cell phone, she thought Keith would call back but he didn't.

Quickly, she retrieved a box from her closet which already had his items neatly packed into it. Then she marched downstairs and placed the box on her front porch. Afterwards, she ran back upstairs to her bedroom. She looked at her clock and realized her date would be arriving in about ninety minutes. She jumped in the shower to get ready.

After almost an hour had passed, Jennifer was almost ready. While in the bathroom, she looked at herself in the mirror then put on her diamond earrings. Now she was complete. All of a sudden, her cell phone began to ring. She exited her bathroom, which was inside her bedroom, and retrieved her phone off the bed. Relieved it was Ashley calling, she quickly answered.

"Hey, sis," she said holding the phone to her ear.

"Hi, Jennifer," Ashley replied back. "What are you doing?"

"I just finished getting ready for my date, with Stewart, tonight. I'm waiting on him to arrive any moment now."

"Oh, that's right, I remember you telling me about your date a few days ago. So where you two headed on a Friday night?"

"He said we could enjoy martinis and a movie at the Fern Bank."

"That sounds interesting, fun, and different."

"Well, what are your plans for tonight, Ashley?"

"Nothing as usual. I'm going to get under the covers and curl up with a good book I just downloaded onto my Kindle."

"What book is that?"

"*Ladies' Man 2* the sequel by Frederick Germaine.

"Oh, girl, you're going to love it. Don't be surprised

if you start playing with yourself under the covers."

"Jennifer behave! You know I don't do that."

"Every woman does now and then, sis. Anyway, if I had known you didn't have plans I would have invited you, with us, for a double date."

"And who was I going to bring as my date?"

"What about your coworker you're always talking about?"

"You mean, Daniel?"

"Yeah, I think that's him."

"He's married, Jennifer."

"Oh, sorry."

"Don't be, it's no big deal. You two have fun and hopefully he won't be a dud like Keith."

"Well, speaking of the devil, he and I are officially over. After I leave, he's picking up a box containing his belonging from my front porch."

"Thank goodness, Jennifer, and good riddance to him."

"Hey, I think I hear Stewart pulling up now," Jennifer said moving towards her bedroom window. "Yes, it's him."

"Okay, I'll talk with you later," said Ashley. "And don't forget to tell me how everything turned out."

By the time the conversation ended between the two sisters, I was ringing the doorbell at the front door. Jennifer rushed to her bathroom mirror for a final look, at herself, then hurried downstairs. When she opened the door, I greeted her with a warm smile and a hug. I also noticed the odd box on the small front porch but said nothing. Soon, she closed the front door and we were off.

Slightly after midnight, we were returning back from the Fern Bank. As I pulled up to the townhome, she noticed something was different. She rushed out of my car and over to her black Cadillac CTS parked in the driveway. Someone had smashed out the driver's side window.

"I can't believe this!" she said yelling out loud.

"Hey, is everything alright?" I asked running up to her.

She said nothing but looked at her prized damaged vehicle in disgust. Then she turned to the front porch and noticed the box was gone. Immediately, she knew who did it. It had to be Keith's crazy ass.

CHAPTER 6

It was Monday morning and Ashley had bypassed her job, in Buckhead, for a more subtle locale on the Southwest side of Atlanta. She was in her old neighborhood where she grew up. On this day, she wanted to give her mother, Mabel, a surprise visit.

"Mom, are you in there?" Ashley asked out loud. Then she repeatedly rang the doorbell. After a while she began to knock thinking the doorbell wasn't working "Mom, it's me Ashley."

She looked at her watched, with a puzzled stare, and wondered where her mother could be. Maybe coming all the way down here was a bad idea, she thought to herself, especially if her mother wasn't home. Just as she was about to depart, a familiar voice calls out.

"Oh, child, if you don't stop making all this ruckus out here," her mother stated sharply as she opened the front door.

"Mom, I was just worried about you," said Ashley.

"I was in the bathroom," said Mabel addressing her daughter. "Well, come on in and make sure you wipe your feet."

"Yes, ma'am," replied Ashley.

After Ashley entered the home, Mabel closed the front door behind her. The two hugged showing their emotional love for each other.

Mabel was a good Christian woman, who spoke with a Southern drawl. She migrated from Mississippi to Georgia, years ago, in search for a better life. Compared to her daughter, she was shorter in stature and slightly overweight. At sixty years old, she had a few health problems including diabetes.

"Ain't you supposed to be at work today?"

"No, mom, I took a half PTO day. I go in at one o'clock."

"A PT who?"

"It's called Paid Time Off, mom. Basically, time off accrued from working."

"Whew, I tell you, I'm already tired," said Mabel as she took a seat on the sofa. "Go ahead, child, and rest your feet."

"Mom, have you been taking your medicine?" asked Ashley taking a seat next to her mother.

"Now, you gonna have to hush, Ashley," said Mabel looking at the small television. "I'm finna watch Judge Mathis and you know that's my favorite show."

"C'mon mom," said Ashley. She looked at the television set, for a split second, then turned back to her mother. "Have you taken your medicine for the day?"

"No, Ashley, I don't think I have."

"Where do you keep your medicine?"

"On the kitchen table."

"Fine, I'll get it for you."

"And fetch me a tall glass of water, too."

"Yes, ma'am."

While her mother immersed herself into *The Judge Mathis Show*, Ashley went into the modest kitchen. She pulled a tall glass from the cabinet and filled it with cold water from the sink's faucet. Then she grabbed her mother's medicine and headed back to the sofa.

Without any hesitation, Mabel popped the pills in her mouth and flushed them down with water. Meanwhile,

Ashley didn't say a word but was satisfied. While her mother's show was on, she strolled over to the fireplace to view the pictures on the mantle. When a commercial came on, she knew it was okay to speak again.

"Mom, I see you still have one of Jennifer's senior high school pictures up here," she said holding the frame in her hand. "This one is when she was crowned Miss Homecoming."

"Yes, Lawd," her mother said looking at her. Mabel then rose from the sofa and joined her daughter at the fireplace. "Ain't she pretty in that picture?"

"Yes, mom, and she still is."

"I was so proud of my baby when that picture was taken."

Ashley placed the cherished memory of her sister back down on the mantle. Then she saw another picture that caught her eye.

"Oh, I didn't know you still had this one of Jennifer," she said picking up another frame.

"I remember that one like it was yesterday," her mother stated. "She was elected president of the student body for her senior class. I was so proud of her."

Yes, we all were," said Ashley.

Mabel noticed a certain look on her daughter's face

41

and wanted to change her expression. She quickly picked up a frame from the mantle and showed it to her daughter.

"Hey, do you remember this one?"

"Yes, mom, that's a picture of me at my senior prom. Wow, look at my hair!"

"Don't you pay that no mind, child. All the young girls were wearing that cute style back in the day."

"Yeah, I guess you're right, mom."

"What ever happened to that nice fella you went to the prom with? I can't seem to remember his name."

"His name was Michael, mom."

"Yes, that's it."

"The last I heard, he made a career for himself in the Army. He got married and had a house full of kids."

"My, my, my ain't that something. Well, speaking about kids, when are you going to have some?"

"Mom, I don't want to talk about that right now."

"Baby, you ain't getting any younger and being in your thirties don't help either. Plus, I want some grandkids before I get too old."

"I'm not having kids just to be having them. I want to be married to a man I love first."

"I don't blame you for that, Ashley. I'm gonna keep praying until the Lord sends you a good God-fearing man."

"Look, mom, Judge Mathis is about to make his ruling," said Ashley pointing at the television. Plus, she wanted to change the subject.

"Oh, child, you got me finna miss the best part," her mother exclaimed. Then she rushed back over to the sofa and took a seat.

As her mother predicted, Judge Mathis ruled in favor of the defendant. Ashley was amused but happy to see her mother enjoying her favorite show. Within a few minutes, another episode came on. Ashley was content on sitting there, watching the show, with the person she loved the most.

CHAPTER 7

It was hump day and I had just finished taking a sizzling hot shower. As I stood there in my large bathroom drying off, I thought about the day that was in front of me. After drying off completely, I wrapped the towel around my waist. Then I moved over to the mirror and sink where I lathered my face in shaving cream. I grabbed my razor and cut all the hair off my entire face. After which, I rinsed my face and splashed on some good-smelling after shave. Momentarily, I stood there in front of the mirror noticing my face was as smooth as a baby's ass. Then I made my way into the bedroom. Before I could remove the towel to get dress, my cell phone on the bed begins to ring. I quickly retrieved it to answer the call.

"Hello," I said already knowing who the caller was.

"Well, good morning, stranger," said the person on the other end.

"Good morning to you, too."

"What are you doing?"

"What do you think I'm doing at seven-thirty on a Wednesday morning? You know I'm getting ready for work."

"Now hold on a minute, Mr. Smarty Pants! You can lose the attitude. I just called to say hello."

"Alright, I'm sorry. I've been under a lot of stress lately at work."

"Let me guess, it's the Luxemburg Group account, right?"

"Yeah, but how did you know?"

"Stewart, I actually listen when you tell me things about your job."

"Guess it slipped my mind I had mentioned it to you."

"It's no problem, baby."

"Hey, I just got out the shower and really need to finish putting my clothes on."

"Wait a minute, are you there with nothing on right now?"

"Nothing except my bath towel wrapped around my waist."

"I bet you know my imagination is running wild right now."

"Well, you're going to have to tame it. I really have to go."

"Okay, I understand but let's meet this weekend for dinner. It's my treat."

"When and where this weekend?"

"Let's say Saturday night at eight-thirty. We can meet at our favorite dinning spot."

"That's sounds good. I'll see you then."

"There's one more thing I need to tell you."

"What's that?"

"Seriously, stop worrying so much about your main account at work. Just like me and you, everything is going to work out fine."

"I hope you're right. I'll see you soon."

"Goodbye, Stewart."

After I disconnected the call, I reached into my dresser and pulled out a pair of boxers and white form-fitting tee shirt. After I put those items on, I went back into the bathroom and brushed my teeth and combed my hair. Then it was time to get fully dressed in my navy blue pinstripe suit. It was conservative, yet dapper enough, for another meeting with the folks from the Luxemburg Group account.

It only took me twenty minutes to arrive at my office located at the corner of Lenox and Peachtree Road. The landmark building had been there for years and the company I worked for was on the tenth floor. After I parked my vehicle in the garage, I took the elevator to my designated floor. When the elevators stopped, I exited and strolled up to a set of reddish-brown doors. I used my security card to gain access through the doors. The first person I saw was the receptionist. I waved to her as she was busy talking on the phone. Finally, I reached my office and took a seat behind the desk. As I turned on my computer, Lauren was buzzing me on my desk phone. Apparently, she saw me walking into my office. Obviously, I took the call.

"Good morning, Lauren," I said quickly.

"Good morning to you, Stewart," she answered back. "I just wanted to give you a brief update."

"Okay, I'm listening."

"Your second meeting with the Luxemburg Group account has been moved up."

"To what time?"

"It's now at eleven-thirty instead of two."

"I can manage that. I'll move some things around but that shouldn't be a problem."

"Also, Mr. Pittman requested to see you once you arrived."

"Did he say for what?"

"He just wanted to discuss your morning meeting in detail."

"Okay, I'm on it. Is there anything else?"

"No, Stewart, not at this moment. But if anything comes up, I'll buzz you."

"Thanks Lauren for all your diligent work. I'll talk with you later."

"You're welcome, Stewart. And good luck with your morning meeting."

After my call ended with Lauren, I stood up from my chair. I straighten my tie as I prepared to walk to Mr. Pittman's office. He was my boss and department head. Our preliminary meeting was just a formality but I still didn't take it lightly. Mr. Pittman was a seasoned gentleman with a no-nonsense approach. If producers wouldn't produce, agents failed to make the sale, or in my case account managers couldn't keep clients paying high dollar premiums they were exiled from the company.

As I began to leave my office, my cell phone rang. I

had a few minutes to spare so I thought I better answer it. Plus, it was someone I had been waiting to hear from.

"Well, good morning, beautiful," I said answering my phone.

"Good morning, Stewart," said Jennifer. I could tell she was smiling now. "How is your day so far?"

"I'm actually on my way to a meeting right now."

"Okay, I won't hold you up. I just wanted to let you know I finally got the window fixed on my car yesterday."

"That's good to hear, Jennifer. I'm sorry you had to deal with such an adolescent act."

"Yeah, me too."

"Did you have any indication who may have done that to your car?"

"I do, Stewart, but I just can't prove it."

"Then maybe you should go to the police."

"I thought about that but they probably can't help anyway."

"And besides, I didn't even have to file an insurance claim since the cost to replace the window was relatively low."

"Well, on a positive note, we must get together soon."

"Yes, I agree, Stewart. The margaritas at the Fern

Bank were fabulous and the movie was good, too."

"I'm really glad you enjoyed everything. So let's say I give you a call later so we can put something down in concrete."

"That sound good. I'll talk with you then."

I was completely satisfied after my short conversation with Jennifer. It would be nice to see her again as well. I suddenly focused back on the matter at hand. Then I straighten my tie again and headed for Mr. Pittman's office.

CHAPTER 8

"Damn, will you just catch the ball next time?" I asked. Then I stared aimlessly into the enormous flat screen in front of me. "I can't believe you didn't haul that one in."

"Hey, buddy, don't get yourself all worked up," announced Luke. After which, he placed another round of popcorn into his mouth. "It's just a preseason NFL football game."

"Yeah, I know but I hate to see my Falcons struggle with these new receivers they drafted."

"They should be fine with the veterans they still have on the team. Besides, the season doesn't start until four weeks from now."

It was Sunday afternoon, in August, and my good friend Luke was visiting me. We had decided to just relax on my couch, in front of the television, while sipping on some brews. Plus, it was scorching hot outside.

I only had a handful of guy friends and Luke was one of them. We had known each other for roughly five years and we were pretty cool. He owned a small construction company and earned a decent income. Ironically, we met when he was doing some contracting work within my condo's building. Eventually, I hired him to fully upgrade my kitchen and we've been pals ever since.

"You're probably right, Luke," I said. Then I put the cold bottle to my lips and took a few sips of beer. "So how's everything going with the construction business?"

"I can't complain," he replied. "I'm picking up new clients all the time since the economy is finally getting better."

"Man, sometimes I wish I could have started my own business."

"Maybe you should because it's never too late. What do you like to do?"

"I like to problem solve, help people, and tackle issues. I think I do a pretty good job of that with my employer."

"You still an account manager for that insurance

company?"

"Yeah, Luke, I'm still with them. I've been there now going on ten years."

"Wow, that's a long time, Stewart. You could stay in the same profession but just branch out and start your own entity."

"Hmmm, that sounds like a good idea. I really might consider doing that next year."

Luke reached in front of me and grabbed some more popcorn from the bowl on the cocktail table. He stuffed his mouth and then washed it down with a cold beer. Of course, by now, the Falcons still couldn't move the ball. I had lost interest in the game altogether.

"Well, speaking about the next year, what are you doing for New Year's Eve?" he asked.

"Luke, it's like a hundred degrees outside," I answered laughing. "I can't begin to think about what I'll be doing for that holiday which is months away."

"I know, Stewart, but my fiancée is already hounding me about the New Year's Eve festivities."

"Why is she pressing you so early?"

"She believes this silly superstition that whoever you bring the new year in with that's who you're going to be with for a long time."

"Man, I never heard that one."

"Yeah, neither have I, Stewart. But since we're getting married next year, she's adamant we should be together for New Year's Eve."

"Okay, I get that, but why is she so anxious on planning it now?"

"You remember last year when we all met at the Loews Hotel in midtown?"

"Yeah, that was a great New Year's Eve party at a ritzy establishment. Plus, you couldn't beat the complimentary champagne and live band."

"That's good because apparently she wants to go to the same venue this year. The only issue is that reservations have to be booked by the first week in September."

"Oh, wow, that will be here before we know it."

"So are you in or out?"

"You can go ahead and count me in, Luke."

"I assume you're bringing the same person as your date from last year. What was her name again?"

"It's Jewell, Luke."

"Yeah, that's it, now I remember. She seemed like a nice young lady when my fiancée and I met her."

"She is but I'm just not into her as I once was when we initially met three years ago."

"How so, Stewart?"

"She has a stable career and pleasant personality but something is just missing with us. And I guess since I met someone else that doesn't help either."

"Seems like you got a case of NPS."

"Huh?"

"It's called New Pussy Syndrome, Stewart. You rather gravitate towards something new and exciting rather than deal with the stable and reliable."

"Seriously, did you just make that one up, Luke?" I asked my friend laughing a little.

"No, Stewart, I didn't," he replied in a serious tone. "Be careful because sometimes new pussy can get you caught up in something serious. Especially if she has blinders on you."

"I hear what you're saying but we seem to click together so well."

"So what's her name anyway?"

"Jennifer is her name."

"Damn, Stewart, even their names are similar."

"Believe me, there's nothing similar about either one of them. Jennifer is a real estate agent with her own company."

"Oh really?"

"Come to think of it, I could even have her refer some of her clients to you. Most people buying or selling homes are always looking to remodel, update, or change something around."

"Man, I think I'm beginning to like this Jennifer person more than Jewell already. But seriously, Stewart, I think you need to disconnect the relationship you're no longer interested in."

"Believe me, I've already thought about that. Plus, it's more complicated than you might imagine. I haven't told you the whole story."

"Well, shoot, I'm ready to hear it. It can't be that bad."

"You sure you want to hear this, Luke?"

"Man, fire away."

I figured we both needed a fresh cold one first. So before I began my story, I got up and headed to the kitchen. I retrieved two beers and popped them open. Then I returned to the couch and handed Luke his beer. I got real comfortable and propped my feet up on the cocktail table. Then I took a sip from my bottle and then another. Finally, I began telling Luke the tight jam I had gotten myself into.

CHAPTER 9

The month of August was almost over and Jennifer was driving to her office. Weather in Atlanta was still hot and so were her sales for the month. She exceeded her monthly goals and was very proud of herself. She continued to travel south on Georgia 400 to her small office located in Roswell on Holcombe Bridge Road. It wasn't too far from her townhome in Alpharetta which made the commute relatively easy.

For years she had worked for a realty company becoming one of the top sales agents. Consistently, she produced yearly sales numbers into the millions making the company very profitable. She was a hot commodity but wanted much more. Eventually, she left the company and decided to start her own. Even though she worked twice as hard, the financial results were worth it.

Now her office didn't have a lot of bells and whistles. It was a small dwelling within a retail strip plaza. To help keep overhead down, she did everything herself. This included answering the phones, sending faxes, marketing her business, and any other day-to-day operations. She stayed busy and when a sale was finalized she reaped all the profits.

Finally, the proud entrepreneur reached her destination. She parked her Cadillac and began walking to her office. As she reached the front door, she read 'Whitaker Realty' etched on the glass door and felt a sense of accomplishment. Once inside, she took a seat and turned her computer on. It was barely eight o'clock and her office phone rang.

"Good morning, Whitaker Realty," she answered in her charming voice. "This is Jennifer, how can I help you?"

"Good morning, Jennifer," replied the pleasant voice on the other end. "My name is Daniel Sims and I was referred by your sister, Ashley. As a matter of fact, we actually work together."

"Oh, hello, Mr. Sims. I'm glad you reached out to me."

"Jennifer, please just call me Daniel. It only seems

fitting since your sister and I are coworkers."

"Okay, Daniel, it is. So what brings you to Whitaker Realty?"

"Well, my wife and I are in the market for a new home."

"Daniel, I can definitely assist you two with your buying needs."

"I feel confidant you can based on what your sister told me."

"That's good to hear," she said grabbing a pen and notepad. "Now, let me gather some basic information from you first."

"Sure, no problem," he said waiting patiently for the next question.

"Now, do you and your wife have a budget in mind?"

"Actually, we qualified for a three-hundred thousand dollar loan."

"And what areas were you two interested in?"

"Somewhere north of the I-75 corridor was what we had in mind. Kennesaw to be exact."

"That's a nice quiet area, Daniel. There has been so much development and growth out there in the last few years."

"Yeah, we currently live in Vinings and are looking for a suburb feel."

"Well, you'll get more home for your dollar in Kennesaw compared to Vinings."

"That really sounds great plus everything we were hoping for, Jennifer."

"How many bedrooms and baths do you two want the home to have?" she asked while still writing on her notepad.

"Um, I'd say a minimum of three bedrooms with at least two bathrooms," he answered. And we would like something with a modern contemporary look."

"I shouldn't have a problem locating your dream home, Daniel. In that area, there are plenty of new construction homes and modern resales."

"Wow, I'm already excited to see what's out there. So where do we go from here?"

"I just need you and your wife to come into my office in Roswell. We need to execute a contract stating I'll be your real estate agent."

"Okay, that shouldn't be a problem. I'll see when she's available and give you a call back."

"That's absolutely fine, Daniel. In the meantime, I'll generate a home portfolio consisting of what you two may like."

"I'm looking forward to see what you came up with.
I'll talk with you soon and thanks a bunch."

"Thank you for trusting me with your home buying
needs. I look forward to servicing you two soon."

The pair hung up and Jennifer felt a sense of relief.
She had secured another client for her ever-growing
business and even her sister had helped. It was while since
Ashley did that but Jennifer was proud anyway. She
quickly made a mental note to call her sister later in the
day.

Within an hour, Jennifer had found a wide range of
homes she thought Daniel and his wife would be interested
in viewing. She printed the listings and placed them in a
binder for her new clients. Before beginning the next
agenda for the day, she decided to call her sister. Quickly,
she picked up the phone's receiver, from the desk, and
dialed the number. Her sister answered right away.

"Hello," said Ashley breathing heavily.

"Hey, sis, is everything alright?" asked Jennifer
sounding concerned.

"Hi, Jennifer, I'm just taking my normal power
walk on my lunch break."

"Well, I didn't mean to interrupt your daily exercise

flow."

"No worries, Jennifer. I can walk and talk at the same time. What's up?"

"I received a call from your coworker, Daniel, this morning."

"Oh, you did?"

"Yes, he and his wife are going to use me as their real estate agent. I just wanted to say thanks for the referral."

"Girl, it's no problem at all. We're sisters and are supposed to look out for each other."

"I know but remind me to take you out for a nice steak dinner or something."

"A steak dinner?"

"Yeah."

"How about half of the commission check once Daniel and his wife close on the house?" asked Ashely laughing a little.

"Okay, we'll see," replied Jennifer laughing herself. "There's one other item I'd like to discuss with you."

"Go ahead, I'm listening."

"What are we going to do for mom on her birthday this year?"

"I don't know, Jennifer, but that date is approaching

soon."

"How about we give her a relaxing day at an exclusive spa with full treatment?"

"We did that for her two years ago."

"Well, what about if we took her out for a nice birthday dinner?"

"Jennifer, you know mom is old-fashioned and would rather have a home cooked meal."

"Yeah, that is true. Let's both think of some birthday ideas and discuss it later."

"That sounds good. I'll call you in a day or so."

"Okay I'll talk with you then."

The two sisters ended their call. Jennifer sat there feeling excited about her new sense of accomplishment. Ashley, on the other hand, continued her power walk breathing heavily.

CHAPTER 10

It had been a few weeks since Luke and I had our in depth conversation. As I was traveling, on the interstate en route to Jewell's house, something he said stood out the most. Maybe I really did have New Pussy Syndrome. I really did care about Jewell but my intuition was telling me to pursue Jennifer.

I had called Jewell earlier letting her know I was coming over after work. I planned on telling her we needed to part ways. Not knowing how she would react to the news, I picked up a single-stem red rose. I figured the flower would symbolize a token of our friendship forever.

I finally found myself pulling off the exit which lead to her home. After traveling a few more miles, I had arrived in her neighborhood. It was an older area of the city but was composed mostly of middle-class inhabitants. All the homes were pretty much ranch style with a few two-story dwellings here and there.

As I pulled into Jewell's driveway, I noticed her next-door neighbor, Mrs. Parker, in her front yard. She was kneeling down working in her flower bed by the mailbox. She was a widow and retired postal worker. Even though she had to be at least twenty-five years older than me, any man could see she was a knockout back in her younger days. She spent most of her days working in her beautifully landscaped yard. Any other time, she spent growing fresh vegetables in her small garden located in the rear of her home.

"Hi, Mrs. Parker," I said as I exited my vehicle. I also waved to her.

"Oh, hello, Stewart," she said looking up. The older, yet vibrant, woman stood up. "How are you doing?"

"I'm doing just fine, ma'am," I answered. "How about yourself?"

"I'm doing very well, Stewart," she answered. "As you can see I'm adding a few new plants within my flower bed."

"Yes, and it seems like you're doing a good job."

"Thank you, Stewart. Come to think about it I haven't seen you in a while."

"Yes, ma'am, I've been busy with work lately logging extra hours for a special project."

"Now, don't you work too hard, dear. Remember, you have to spend quality time with the ones you love."

"I'll try to keep that in mind. Well, I'm going to head inside now, I'll see you around."

"Okay, Stewart, I'll talk with you next time."

As I moved beyond my car and walked up to Jewell's front porch, Mrs. Parker kneeled back down. She went back to tending to her well-put-together flowers. Meanwhile, I rang Jewell's doorbell.

"Hey, baby," Jewell said with a bright smile. Then she hugged me before I could get through the front door completely. "I'm so glad you decided to come by."

"Yeah, so am I, "I said lying to her.

"Is that rose for me?" she asked after closing the front door.

"Yes, it is," I answered as I extended it to her. "It's just a little something I picked up on my way over here."

"Oh, you're so sweet, Stewart. Go ahead and take a seat while I finish cooking dinner."

I paused and looked around the older ranch style

home. As usual, it was clean and tastefully decorated like always. In the air was a sweet aroma of Southern cooking. Before following her instructions, I decided to speak again.

"You didn't have to go through all that, Jewell. Like I mentioned earlier on the phone, I just wanted to talk."

"Don't be silly, Stewart. You've been working hard all day and need a good home cooked meal. And besides, I like to cook."

"You're not listening to me, Jewell."

"I cooked fried pork chops smothered in brown mushroom gravy, fresh boiled corn on the cob, and sweet potatoes just the way you like them."

"Stop it, Jewell."

"Okay, Stewart, just spit it out! What do you have to say?"

"You know it's not working out between us, Jewell. I've been feeling this way for a while now."

"So you let that bitch come between us, Stewart?" she asked while shouting. Then she took the rose and struck it across my chest. "And what the hell is this damn rose for?"

"It doesn't mean I don't care about you, Jewell," I answered.

"I told you when all this started she didn't have to

know about us. Now you're reneging on our agreement, huh?"

"Jewell, I have a right to change my mind if I choose."

"Not if you made a promise to me, Stewart."

"Please, let's not go there."

"Does she really satisfy you better than me?"

"You know I'm not going to answer that question."

Jewell quickly took both of her hands and pushed my chest until my back was against the front door. She stood in my path so I had nowhere to go. Then she squatted down and began to unbuckle my belt.

"C'mon, Jewell, I didn't come over here for that."

"Shhhh, baby, momma wants to know the answer to her question."

She calmly unloosen the button and zipper to my slacks. Then she pulled them, along with my boxers, down to my ankles. I stood there not saying another word.

She just put the head of my dick into her warm mouth teasing me. Then she took it out and licked my dick, all over, fast and repeatedly with her tongue. While this was going on, she massaged my balls and even licked them too. Within seconds, my dick was rock hard saluting her. She placed me into her warm juicy mouth slowly going in and out. As she did this, she kept her eyes looking up at me. It was turning me on so bad I moaned out loud and flung my head back. She stroked my hard dick with her mouth over and over again until I was almost there. I was about to bust in her mouth when I cried out.

"Damn, that shit feels so good!"

"I'm not letting you off the hook that easy," she proudly said after removing my dick from her mouth. "And besides, I still want you to answer my question."

She stood up while still looking into my eyes. I bent down and pulled my boxers and slacks up to my waist again. Then she grab my hand and led the way to her bedroom. We made a quick detour, through the kitchen, where she turned the stove and oven completely off.

About an hour later, she was laying on my chest silently sleeping. She had rode me very well like the fine stallion she was. She came twice and I once. I had one arm around her as I looked at the ceiling fan above us. The mahogany blades were slowing turning as the Southern cooking aroma was still in the air.

PART II

A WOLF AMONG US

CHAPTER 11

"Next point wins," I said breathing hard.

"Yeah, I know," Luke responded in his best defensive stance. "But I bet you can't get around me."

"Don't get too cocky, you know I got a quick first step."

"And I've been known to play some helluva defense. Let's see what you got."

It was a cool fall Sunday afternoon. Luke and I were outside, at a park near my home, playing a game of one-on-one basketball. The intensity of the game had picked up and you could see it in both of our eyes.

Just as he dared me to make a move, I took him up on his offer. We were both at the free throw line when I made a quick dart towards the basket. With him barely in front of me, I dribbled the ball through my legs and sprinted right. As he beat me to the ball, I crossed over and changed directions going left. Suddenly, I was past him with nothing but the goal in front of me. After a few more dribbles, I leaped up laying the basketball towards the rim knowing I had the game won. Out of nowhere, he recovers and swats the ball as it leaves my hand. The bright orange rubber object ricochets off the backboard and bounces towards the three-point line. I chased after the ball with him in front of me. As he corralled the ball, I took my own best defense stance in front of him.

"You can't get around me," I said. My knees were bent and both of my arms were extended sideways. "You're not as fast as me and that was a lucky block."

"I don't need to be as fast as you," he announced holding the ball. "I just need to be more skillful."

"Then take your best shot."

"You sure about that, Stewart."

"Yeah."

As soon as I dared him, he hoisted up a jumper from roughly thirty feet out. I jumped up trying to alter his shot but it was too late. The ball had left his hand in perfect form. I turned in the opposite direction to see where it

would land. As I did, it passed through the rim, hitting
nothing but net.

"Game over!"

"Damn, Luke, you beat me again."

We both shook each other hands as a sign of good
sportsmanship. With both of us winded, we decided to
catch our breath for a moment. We sat on the black asphalt
next to the fence which enclosed the court. I pulled out two
Gatorade bottles from my sports bag and gave one to him.

"You're not quite that old yet," I said. Then I helped
myself to a few gulps from the bottle. "Wait till about
twenty years from now."

"I guarantee you by then I won't be caught on the
basketball court."

"Yeah, same here."

"Man, what are we doing out here anyway?" Luke
asked. "We need to be inside by your flat screen since the
NFL season just kicked off."

"The Falcons don't play until Monday night," I
answered. "Plus, all this cardio workout is good for us."

"Yeah, I guess you're right, Stewart," he said. "So
did you ever take care of that dilemma you were in?"

"Not really," I answered. "But believe me I tried."

"Did you really?"

"Yes, I did. I even went over to Jewell's house recently to break things down to her. But we end up having sex anyway."

"Damn, that's some POP shit for you."

"Man, you and your acronyms. Please enlighten me on what POP stand for?"

"It's the Power of the Pussy, Stewart."

"You can't be serious about that one, Luke."

"I'm dead serious, Stewart. Seems like Jewell has you by the balls with her sweet juices."

"No, believe me, it's not like that."

"Then how so?"

"Well, we made an agreement a while ago. Now, I'm backing out on what I agreed to do."

"Was the agreement in writing?"

"Man, you know it wasn't."

"In my line of work, if it's not in writing then there is no agreement, Stewart."

We both continued to catch our breath while sipping on Gatorade. The much needed rest after a competitive game of pickup basketball was doing us both some good. Later, Luke even struck up a conversation about a new contract he secured. I was happy for him as his business continued to grow. With the sun beginning to set and the temperature dropping, I made a suggestion to my good friend.

"How about another game?" I asked.

"I see you still think you can beat me," he said standing up. He picked up the basketball and tossed it to me. "You're on, Stewart, losers always take out the ball first."

I cracked a smile knowing I had a slim chance of prevailing against him. It was just my competitive nature that made me want to play again. I stood up and took a deep breath. Luke took his normal defensive stance in front of me. Then I began to dribble as we both commenced another game of one-on-one basketball.

CHAPTER 12

It was high noon and Ashley has just completed her power walk ritual during her lunch break. Today, she pushed herself even further by going three extra city blocks. She felt great with her new achievement for the day.

While entering the building, she noticed construction for a new business in the lobby was almost finalized. Up until now, there was brown paper covering the glass windows as to not let anyone see what was being built on the inside. A few workers had removed the covering so she decided to ease over to see what was going on.

"Fitness World," she said out loud to herself

reading the glass.

"That's right," said a firm voice from her back. "And our motto is: We'll work you out until you're fit."

Caught off guard, she quickly turned around. She was pleased at what was in front of her. Standing there was a tall, dark, and handsome man. He had to be at least six-three weighing two-hundred and thirty pounds. His body was perfectly chiseled without any sight of irregularity. Plus, his chest and arms were almost bursting out of the tee shirt he was wearing. To top it off, she noticed a nice size bulge in the front of the shorts he had on.

"Oh my," she exclaimed.

"Sorry, I didn't mean to startle you," he said.

"It's no problem at all," she said smiling.

"Hi, I'm Apollo," he said offering his right hand. "I'm actually the franchisee for this new location."

"Nice to meet you, Apollo," she said shaking his hand. "I'm Ashley and I work on the seventh floor."

"Seventh floor, huh?"

"Yes, that's right."

"The energy company is on that floor if I'm correct."

"You're absolutely right."

"I actually just came down from that floor. I gave

the receptionist a few postcards regarding my new gym down here in the lobby."

"I'll be sure to mention it to a few of my colleagues as well."

"I appreciate that, Ashley. So do you work out on a regular basis?"

"As a matter of fact, I just finished up my daily power walk on my lunch break. I'm pretty sure you can see I'm still trying to lose a few pounds."

"Ashley, you look fine to me. Personally, I like a little meat and potatoes within my diet."

Apollo's comments caught Ashley by surprised. She blushed not knowing what to say next. Before she could say anything, her coworker interrupts her thoughts.

"There you are, Ashley," said Daniel approaching the pair. "I was waiting for you to come back upstairs. I figured you may want to go grab something to eat."

"No thanks, Daniel," she stated. "I normally just eat some yogurt after my walk."

"Okay, I'll see you in a bit, Ashley," Daniel said.

"Oh, by the way, I want to introduce you to someone," she announced proudly. "This is Apollo, he's the owner of the new Fitness World that just opened here in the lobby."

"Nice to meet you, Apollo," said Daniel extending his hand.

"Likewise, Daniel," said Apollo shaking his hand.

"I've been seeing a lot of these Fitness Worlds sprouting up all over the city."

"Yeah, the company has a big campaign to put locations in various areas with high emphasis on office buildings. Here, Daniel, take a postcard as you may want to consider joining."

"Thanks, Apollo, I'll give it some serious thought."

"Now remember to eat healthy on your lunch break"

"After looking at your body, I feel compelled to."

Daniel finally said goodbye to the two and headed out the front entrance. Meanwhile, Apollo turned his attention back to Ashley and continued their conversation.

"You know, Ashley, after your walk you should eat something healthier."

"So you don't endorse me eating yogurt, huh?"

"Not really. You should trying something more nutritional within your diet."

"Like what?"

"I would suggest leafy green vegetables like a salad or even fruit."

"Hmmm, thanks for the dietary tip, Apollo."

"Besides being an owner, I'm a personal trainer as well. I'd love to get you in my gym for a workout."

"Maybe that can be arranged. Sometimes just walking can be a bit monotonous."

"Here, take one of my business cards," he said. "I'm available seven days a week at just about any hour.

"Yes, I'll keep that in mind," she said glancing at his card.

"Would you like to take a quick tour through our gym facility?"

"Mmm, I'd love to but I really have to get back upstairs."

"Okay, maybe some other time."

"Yes, I'm pretty sure real soon."

"Keep in mind we have state-of-the-art equipment, a sparkling indoor pool, plus a professional and friendly environment."

"I definitely will, Apollo. I have to go now but I look forward to seeing you soon."

"As do I. Enjoy the rest of your day, Ashley."

Ashley simply smiled and walked towards the elevators. As she did, Apollo continued to observe her physique. She glanced again at the business card in her hand. After walking a few extra city blocks, getting a compliment on her figure, and meeting her potential personal trainer today was turning out to be a good day.

CHAPTER 13

"I think you missed the turn, Daniel," said Terri to her husband.

"No, I didn't," he responded back. "The GPS states we're to continue traveling south on Holcombe Bridge Road."

"Are you sure?"

"Yes, I'm positive, Terri."

"I just don't want us to get lost. There's so much traffic on this road."

"Don't worry, we won't."

"I can't wait until we move into our new home away from all this hustle and bustle of the city life."

"That makes two of us."

The GPS navigation system inside their vehicle gave instructions for him to take a right turn a few feet away. He turned his signal on and began to press the brakes a little slowing down the car.

"You were right, Daniel. Apparently, we didn't miss our turn."

"We should be at Jennifer's office any moment now."

He continued to drive but at a slower pace. Within minutes, he turned into the plaza where Jennifer's office was located and found a parking spot. Then he exited the vehicle and walked around to the passenger side door.

"C'mon, honey, we're finally here," he said opening his wife's door. "Take my hand so I can help you out the car."

"Oh, Daniel, you're so sweet," she said. "You don't have to do all that."

"We can never be too cautious especially since you're carrying our future."

"Yes, I guess you're right."

Still holding her hand, he led his wife to Jennifer's office which was only a few yards away. When the pair arrived at the front door, he opened it for her. She entered first as he followed behind her.

"Well, good afternoon you two," said Jennifer greeting her guests at the front door.

"Hello," said Daniel back to her. "Are you Jennifer?"

"Yes, I am."

"It's good to finally meet you, I'm Daniel."

"It's my pleasure meeting you, Daniel," said Jennifer as the two shook hands.

"I'd like for you to meet my wife, Terri," he said turning to his significant other.

"Hi, Terri, it's nice meeting you as well," Jennifer said now shaking her hand.

"Hello, Jennifer," she said.

Suddenly, without notice, Terri held her head down as if she didn't feel well. Jennifer noticed it first.

"Terri, are you feeling okay?" Jennifer asked.

"I don't really know, Jennifer," she replied. "All of a sudden, I feel light-headed and woozy."

"Honey, maybe you need to sit down and rest for a second," said Daniel sounding concerned.

"Yes, let's all move closer to my desk," suggested Jennifer. "I have a comfortable chair you can sit in, Terri."

Jennifer led the way to her large desk where she conducted all of her business. There she pointed out a plush chaise lounge were Terri could relax. Daniel quickly took a seat next to his wife.

"My doctor said I would begin to have these symptoms during the early stages of my pregnancy," said Terri sounding a little embarrassed.

"Well, congratulations on your pregnancy, Terri," said Jennifer. "How far along are you?"

"Four months now," she replied.

"Honey, maybe you should try to drink something while you're sitting down," suggested Daniel.

"I think that's a good idea," said Jennifer. I have some chilled bottle water in the refrigerator."

"That sound refreshing, Jennifer," said Terri. "I believe I'll take one."

Jennifer hurried off to the area of her office where she kept a small refrigerator. Within it, she kept refreshments for her clients. Quickly, she grabbed a bottled water and returned back to her guests.

"Here you are, Terri," said Jennifer handing her the bottle.

"Thank you, Jennifer," she said taking possession of it.

"Honey, maybe we should reschedule if you're not feeling well," said Daniel.

"I'm fine, Daniel," she said to her husband. "It's no big deal, we can continue."

By now, Jennifer had moved to the chair which was positioned behind her large desk. She calmly sat down and opened a folder in front of her. After grabbing the document she then turned back to the couple in front of her.

"I took the liberty of preparing an agreement between us," she said. "It basically outlines my fees as I represent you two as your real estate agent."

"Okay," said Daniel retrieving the document. "Just give us a few moments to overlook the agreement."

"By all means," responded Jennifer. "Please, take your time and let me know if you have any questions."

The happy couple thoroughly read through the agreement. They even had a few questions that Jennifer was able to answer for them. After a few more minutes, the agreement had been executed by all parties.

"Now that we have that out the way, we're anxious to see what you have found for us," announced Terri.

"I think you'll be quite impressed on what I was able to locate for you two," said Jennifer.

She took another folder from her desk and placed it in front of them. It contained a listing of homes, with photos, and other pertinent information. Daniel quickly opened the folder while his wife looked on.

"Oh, wow, look at these homes," he said with excitement. He continued to flip through the listings. "They are so spacious and gorgeous."

"I can't wait until we go out and view them," said Terri looking on with her husband.

"You know I usually advise my clients to review their portfolio for a few days before going out for a showing," said Jennifer. "But in your case, I'm willing to show you homes today if you see something you like."

"Jennifer, are you sure it won't be a problem if we wanted to view homes today? Daniel asked.

"It won't be a problem at all, Daniel," she answered. "Actually, you two are my last clients I had booked for this Saturday afternoon. So I'm free to accommodate you both."

"Well, now I'm really getting excited," exclaimed Terri.

"I'll drive and you two can relax and ride with me," suggested Jennifer. "Just let me know which home you like to view so I can plan the route."

The couple loved her suggestion. Momentarily, all three of them were walking out the office headed towards Jennifer well-cleaned Cadillac. Daniel and Terri quickly realized their dream of owning a home was about to come true.

CHAPTER 14

It was Saturday evening and I had another hot date with Jennifer. As usual, she couldn't decide what to wear even though she had clothes falling out of her closet. Ashely, who had arrived at her sister's home an hour earlier, was attempting to help her make the right selection. She sat on the edge of the bed as Jennifer was changing into another outfit in her enormous walk-in closet.

"C'mon out and let me see your ensemble," yelled Ashley.

"Give me a second, Ashely," Jennifer yelled back. "I'm on my way but I had to pull down my skirt."

She emerged from the closet and walked directly in front of her sister. There she did a pirouette and finished it

89

off by placing her hand upon her waist. She said nothing while waiting for her sister's approval.

"I don't like it," said Ashley shaking her head from side to side.

"What do you mean you don't like it?" asked Jennifer removing her hand from her waist.

"It's a nice skirt and top but it doesn't stand out, Jennifer."

"Well, I'm tired of trying on outfits. This is my eighth one already."

"You said Stewart was planning on taking you out on a romantic dinner, right?"

"Yeah, that's what he said. Although, he didn't tell me exactly where."

"Then return the favor and give him an even bigger surprise."

"What do you mean, Ashley?"

"Girl, put on something sexy, seductive, and sinful that will keep his imagination running wild all night long."

"And this is coming from my sister who doesn't have a date, yet again, on a Saturday night."

"That's because I choose not to, Jennifer. And besides, I know how to turn a man on."

"Okay, I do have something that's very eye-catching but I was saving it for a special occasion."

"Jennifer, this is a special occasion. Now, go grab the outfit from your closet and let me see it."

Jennifer did as her sister requested. She promptly marched back into her closet and retrieved the special occasion outfit. With the dress still on the hanger, she walked back in front of Ashley.

"Well, what do you think?" she asked holding the dress up to her gorgeous body.

"Now, that's a dress to kill for," he sister replied. "I love the light shade of red."

"Ashley, I know he'll love how this dress shows just enough cleavage, curves, and, of course, my ass."

"Believe me, Jennifer, every man in the venue will especially like that. Now put the dress on because I want to see you in it."

Jennifer hurried off to her closet again as she did previously. There she removed the outfit she was wearing and replaced it with the dress her sister loved so much. While she stood in the closet, Ashley's phone began to chime. Her sister retrieved the phone and read the text message. Then she responded and stuffed the phone back into her purse.

"So how do I look?" Jennifer asked exiting the

closet.

"You look absolutely beautiful in that dress," answered Ashley.

"Thanks, sis, now please help me find a pair of sexy heels to compliment my dress."

"You can't be serious, Jennifer. There are at least a hundred pair of shoes in your closet."

"That's why I need your help, Ashley."

"Seriously, I have to go now," said Ashley grabbing her purse.

"Where are you going so soon?" asked Jennifer.

"My neighbor just texted me. She needs me to babysit her daughter earlier instead of later this evening."

"So you're not going to be here to meet Stewart when he arrives?"

"I'm sorry, Jennifer, I guess not. I'll have to meet him some other time."

"Well, can you at least stay a few more minutes and help me with my makeup and hair?"

"Yeah, I guess so since you're running behind trying on all these outfits."

The two sisters headed into the large bathroom which was connected to the bedroom. Ashley gave her sister a suggestion on how to style her hair differently. It was sort of a new look to keep Stewart impressed and in awe. Then she assisted with Jennifer's makeup. She didn't need much because her beauty was overwhelming and so natural. After twenty minutes, Jennifer was looking quite breathtaking.

"Thanks for suggesting the new hair style," said Jennifer looking in the mirror. "I think Stewart will like the new look."

"I'm certain he will," stated Ashley.

"And I couldn't have put on my makeup the way you did."

"It's no problem. Now I really have to go."

"Okay, I'll walk you downstairs."

Jennifer did just that and at the front door gave her younger sister a hug and kiss. After Ashley departed, she hurried back upstairs to her bathroom. She tightened up her hair a bit and then moved back into her closet. There she found the perfect pair of alluring four-inch heels not every woman could wear. Then she slipped them onto her feet and waited for her night to begin.

CHAPTER 15

It was barely after seven o'clock when I arrived at Jennifer's townhome in Alpharetta. I eagerly pulled into her driveway and parked my car. Then I grabbed the dozen red roses, which were eloquently wrapped in paper, from the passenger side seat. As I walked to the front door, I made sure my slacks, jacket, and well-pressed shirt were intact. After I confirmed my attire was fine, I rang the doorbell.

Meanwhile, upstairs, Jennifer was still in the bathroom mirror making sure she looked flawless. After hearing the doorbell chime, she sprayed on some expensive perfume and headed for the door. While walking downstairs, she took her time as she didn't want to fall in her high-end four-inch heels. Then she put a perfect smile upon her face and answered the door.

"Well, hello there, Stewart," she said

"Good evening, Jennifer," I said hiding the roses behind my back.

"You look very distinguished."

"Thank you and you look quite attractive in that magnificent dress."

"I appreciate the compliment. Please, come on in."

I followed Jennifer's instruction and entered her home. As she closed the door, I turned slightly still holding the roses behind my back. After she finished securing the front door, we stood face to face in the foyer.

"These are for you," I said removing the roses from my back.

"Oh, my goodness, Stewart, they are beautiful," she exclaimed. Then she took possession of the roses. "And they're in full bloom too."

"Come to think about it, they complement your lovely dress."

"Yes, I guess you're right."

"How did you know red is my favorite color?"

"I didn't, Stewart. Actually, my sister Ashley helped me pick out this dress."

"Well, I definitely have to thank her. Where is she

anyway?"

"Unfortunately, she's not here."

"I thought you were going to introduce us this evening?"

"Yes, Stewart, that was the plan. Apparently, she had to leave for some unexpected business."

"That's not a problem. There's always next time."

"Yes, you're right. Now, come have a seat in the living room while I find a vase for these wonderful roses."

"Okay, I'm right behind you."

Jennifer led the way as I followed. While she walked ahead of me, my eyes were glued on her sexy ass as it swayed from side to side. I tried to keep my composure but devilish thoughts were running through my mind. When we reached the living room, I took a seat. She continued on to the kitchen. I sat there momentarily then she reappeared.

"Now, where did you say we are going this evening for dinner?" Jennifer asked. She placed the vase, with the roses in them, on the cocktail table.

"I didn't say," I replied.

"That's right you didn't," she said taking a seat next to me. "I thought maybe I could get you to slip up."

"Nice try, Jennifer, but you'll have to wait for the

surprise."

"That's fine, Stewart. I like surprises anyway."

"Hey, it's a quarter after seven," I said looking at my watch. "We need to be there by seven forty-five."

"I'm ready," she responded. "Let me just grab my purse."

Jennifer hurried away as she was excited to find out where we were going. When she returned to the living room, with her small purse, I stood up. Together we walked to the front door. She turned out all the lights before we exited her home.

I drove at a steady pace while Jennifer sat comfortably in the passenger's side seat. We made small talk over the Pandora station playing classic R&B tunes. After a twenty-five minute drive, and some stop-and-go traffic, we reached our destination on Powers Ferry Road in Atlanta.

"Here we are," I announced pulling up to the valet. "I hope you like the surprise."

"You made a great choice in selecting this venue for tonight," she said. "It's actually one of my favorite establishments."

"I hope you haven't been out here too much."

"Actually, I don't get out here enough. I love the

surprise, Stewart."

She unbuckled her seatbelt and leaned over to my side. Without warning, she gave me a kiss on my lips. I was caught off guard and before I could say anything the valet opened my door.

"Good evening, sir," he said holding my door open for me. "Welcome to Ray's on the River."

"Good evening to you as well," I said getting out the vehicle.

"Hope you have a wonderful time dining with us tonight, sir," he said handing me a ticket.

"I'm sure I will," I said as I took the small white object.

By now, another valet had opened Jennifer's door. He escorted her to where I stood. She wrapped her arm around me as we both walked into the establishment.

Once inside, we were greeted by a friendly young woman. I told her I had a special reservation. Within seconds, someone was leading the way to our linen top table. After we were seated, I noticed a chilled bottled of champagne I had preordered. A well-dressed gentleman came up to our table and greeted us. Then he poured Jennifer and me a glass of champagne. The ambiance was perfect as a few feet away a live jazz band was playing softly. I advised the gentlemen we would order a few minutes later. He understood and departed our table.

"Before I make a toast, I would like to extend an invitation to you," I said.

"Another surprise I assume," she said back.

"I guess you can say that."

"Well, I'm listening."

"I would be honored if you accompany me to a New Year's Eve party at the Loews Hotel."

"You mean the yearly party in midtown everyone always talks about."

"Yes, that's the one."

"I've never had the luxury of attending."

"Well, now you do. So what's your answer?"

"Of course I will."

"As you probably know, it's a formal event and we're bound to have a lot of fun."

"I'd love to get dressed up and bring in the new year with you."

"We will also be joined by my good friend and his fiancée."

"That's even better. I'm so excited even though New Year's Eve is a few months away."

"Now, let me propose a toast," I said holding my

glass of champagne up in the air a little.

"Sure thing," she said joining her glass with mine.

"For good times to come between us today, tomorrow, and furthermore."

"I agree."

We touched our glasses and then took a sip to memorialize the toast. Later, we feasted on seafood which included lobster, shrimp, and crab. I was happy my surprise to Jennifer went well. But more importantly, I was relieved I had secured my date for the New Year's Eve party.

CHAPTER 16

"C'mon, mom, blow out the birthday candles on your cake," said Ashley standing next to her mother.

"Oh, child, you know I ain't a bit of good doing that with my emphysema and all," said Mabel seated at the table with her cake in front of her.

"We'll help you, mom," announced Jennifer who was standing on her mother's opposite side. "Let's all blow out the candles together on my count of three."

The trio leaned forward towards the candles, atop the cake, and blew as hard as they could. As expected, every candle on the cake was fully extinguished.

"So what did you wish for, mom?" asked Jennifer.

"To have my beautiful daughters around me on my

birthday," she answered.

"Oh, that's so sweet, mom," said Ashley. "We love you."

Simultaneously, the two daughters hugged their mother and gave her a kiss. Mabel tried to hold her composure and fight off the tears but streaks ran down her face. She quickly wiped them away.

"Aw, mom, don't you start crying now," her eldest daughter proclaimed. "Otherwise, you're going to have me getting emotional too."

"Jennifer, you know I can't help it," said Mabel. "I'm glad y'all didn't forget me on my birthday."

"Mom, you would never have to worry about that," said Ashley rubbing her mother's back.

"Well, we might as well dig in," said Mabel. "This is a day we all get to cheat on our diet."

"I'll grab the plates and forks," said Jennifer.

"Okay, I'll get the bowl and spoons for the ice cream," added Ashley.

Momma Mabel did the honors of cutting the cake. She gave Jennifer the first slice then Ashley the next one. She cut herself a small piece even though the cake was sugar-free to combat her diabetes. Ashley put two scoops of Vanilla ice cream in everyone's bowl. As you might have guessed, the frozen dessert was sugar-free as well. The three of them dug into their sweets without saying a word. Finally, Mabel broke the silence.

"So I hear you're dating someone new nowadays," said Mabel.

"How did you find out about that?" asked Jennifer looking at her sister

"I have ways of finding things out, baby," answered her mother proudly.

"Well, since you mentioned it, I'm actually seeing someone new."

"Lawd o' mercy, I hope he's better than that Keith character you use to date."

"Mom, please! Ashley yelled out.

"I'm just being truthful, Ashley."

"Yes, mom, I'd admit he's much better than Keith."

"Now, what's his name and what does he do?"

"His name is Stewart and he's an account manager for a major insurance company."

"I see you chose a corporate man this time around, huh?"

"Yes, mom, he does have a nice job and dresses well."

"I just hope he's the right one for you, Jennifer,"

said Mabel. "Because ain't nann one of y'all getting any younger. Plus, I want some grandkids around here before I get too old."

"Oh, mom, that will happen when it's supposed to," added Jennifer. "Despite what you might think, Ashley and I still have plenty of time."

"So how did your last date with Stewart turn out?" Ashley asked getting off the subject of grandkids.

"It was great," replied Jennifer. "He surprised me with an intimate dinner at Rays on the River. Then he invited me to a New Year's Eve party at the Loews Hotel in midtown."

"You mean the upscale party everyone wants to go to every year?" Ashley asked.

"Yes, that's the one," answered her sister.

"Ol' folks back in Mississippi used to say the man you bring in the new year with was the man you were gonna be with,"

"Is that old saying really true, mom?" Ashley asked.

"Hey, let's stop talking about me," said Jennifer before her mother could answer. "Mom, it's all about you today. Therefore, we wanted to surprise you with a getaway trip for a day."

"We booked an all-inclusive day and night, for your

enjoyment, at Callaway Gardens," added Ashley.

"Calla who?" Mabel asked.

"C'mon now, mom, you've heard of Callaway Gardens," said Jennifer. "It's right outside of Columbus and only a forty-five minute drive from here."

"Child, you know I'm old fashioned," stated Mabel. "I don't ever stay away from my home."

"Mom, it's something different we want you to experience," said Ashley. "Plus, we've already paid for everything in advance."

"I guess I'll have to make an exception this time," said Mabel reluctantly. "Especially since y'all done paid your hard-earned money on me."

All three women raised up from the table together. Ashley volunteered to stay in the kitchen and wash the dishes. Jennifer followed Mabel into her bedroom. There the pair picked out a few outfits and neatly packed them into an overnight bag.

In less than an hour, everyone was ready to go. The sisters told their mother how much they loved her. Mabel expressed her love right back at them. Before they exited the front door, Mabel made her daughters bow their heads. She said a short prayer asking for a safe travel and also thanked God for another blessed birthday.

CHAPTER 17

It was Friday evening around five-thirty and I was exhausted from working all week. I picked up a new account and, of course, they needed to be pacified a little. All I could think about was going home and cracking open a cold beer in front of the flat screen. I grabbed my sports jacket, leather portfolio, and keys off my desk before I headed to the elevator. Everyone had departed the office including Lauren. The only visible people were a few members of the cleaning staff as they began their tasks.

As I exited the elevator, I paused momentarily and put on my jacket. I could see through the large glass doors, in the lobby, it was quite breezy outside. It was windy for an early November evening.

"Mr. Sellers, I'm glad I caught you," said Solomon as I walked out of the building. "I tried to call you, in your office, upstairs by got no answer."

"What's going on, Solomon?" I asked buttoning up my jacket.

Solomon was a retiree who worked part-time in the parking garage. He basically patrolled the grounds making sure everything was okay. Everyone seemed to get along with him because he was very friendly.

"There was a young lady here to see you a few minutes ago. She claimed you were expecting her."

"Oh, really?"

"Yes, sir. I tried to get her drivers' license, at the gate entrance, so I could give her a visitor's pass. She refused and simply drove through the entrance which was open."

"What's her name?"

"Um, I'm not sure, Mr. Sellers. But she did say she would wait for you at your reserved parking spot."

"Okay, Solomon, I can handle it from here."

"Do you need me to walk you to your car?"

"That's not necessary. I should be alright."

"I'll be making my normal rounds in the parking garage soon. If you need anything just let me know."

"Sure thing, Solomon."

The sun was setting and the wind was picking up more as I walked onwards. I went up a flight of stairs and found my car still in its reserved parking spot. Facing my car, and parked a few spaces away, I noticed Jewell waiting for me. She sat in her car motionless with the engine still running. I decided to walk over to her car to see what was really going on.

"What's all this commotion about, Jewell?" I asked once I reached her car. She suddenly let down her window nearly all the way.

"I can't believe what you did and how you're treating me, Stewart," she answered in an angry tone.

"I don't know what you're talking about, Jewell."

"Dammit, you don't answer my calls or texts! So this is how you end three years with me?"

"Listen, Jewell, the last time I was over your house, to talk, you ignored me. You thought fucking and sucking me would make everything alright."

"Don't act like you didn't enjoy every minute of it, Stewart. And besides, I didn't hear you asking me to stop."

"It's been official there's no more you and I."

"What did you just say?"

"You heard me, Jewell."

"What about the agreement we made, Stewart?"

"I guess I'm reneging on that because all bets are off."

"Go to hell, Stewart!"

I knew if I continued to communicate with Jewell our heated conversation would only escalate. So I decided to simply remove myself from the equation. Saying nothing more, I turned away from her and began walking to my car. As I did, she continued to yell at me.

Suddenly, I heard her car's engine revved up behind me but I kept walking. Then I heard tires peeling out on the pavement and I was compelled to turn around. When I did, I saw Jewell's car coming straight for me. At the last second, I lunged sideways on the hood of my car. She barely missed me but nicked the front quarter panel of my Mercedes. She didn't slow down one bit as she turned the corner leading out of the parking garage.

"Mr. Sellers, are you okay?" Solomon asked running up to my car.

"I think so," I answered removing myself from the hood.

"That crazy woman could have killed you."

"Yeah, I know."

"I'm going to call the police for you," he said

removing a cell phone from his pocket.

"That won't be necessary," I calmly said still clutching my portfolio in one hand. Then I took my other hand and began straightening out my clothes.

"What do you mean, Mr. Sellers?" Solomon asked with a perplexed look. "She couldn't have gotten too far from here."

"I'm saying the police won't be needed, Solomon," I firmly replied. "And I'm not even injured at all."

"But your car is damaged, sir."

"It's drivable and no big deal. Plus, my insurance will take care of the damages."

"Mr. Sellers, this doesn't seem right. What's really going on?"

"Listen, Solomon, I'm going to get in my car and drive home. As far as you and I are concerned, nothing happened in this parking garage."

"Okay, sir, if you say so."

"Enjoy your weekend and I'll see you next week."

Solomon moved out of my way, and said nothing, as I walked to my car's door. Once it was open, I flung my portfolio inside and sat down. As I drove off, Solomon continued to look confused.

When I arrived home, I went straight for the

refrigerator. I removed a cold beer and retrieved a bottle opener from the drawer. Then I thought for a second and left the beer on the counter. I moved over to the cabinet where I stashed all my liquor. I pulled out a bottle of top-shelf cognac and a shot glass. Seconds later, I poured myself a drink, then another, and another. The only thing I could think about was how Jewell tried to kill me and what I needed to do next.

CHAPTER 18

It was another routine Monday at the energy company where Ashley worked. She was seated at her desk going through some paperwork when her coworker strolled up to her.

"Hey, you seem sort of down today," said Daniel. "How's everything going?"

"Well, for starters, it's Monday," she answered. "And the fact that Charlene wants me to recalculate the numbers, for a stack of invoices, won't make the day any better."

"Ouch, that's got to hurt. I'm sorry she stuck you with all that work."

"It's no problem, Daniel. I guess a lot of work is

better than no work. So how's your day going?"

"Good so far. I'm just about caught up with everything this morning."

"Well, lucky for you."

"I just wanted to stop by and let you know your sister is pretty awesome."

"Daniel, I told you so. How's the house hunting turning out?"

"It's really going good."

"I'm anxious to see what you and Terri found so far."

"You're in luck, Ashley," he said holding up a small electronic device. "I brought my tablet into work today to show you a few homes."

"Then pull up a chair, Daniel," she said while looking around momentarily.

"Are you sure since you're slammed with a lot of work and all?"

"Yes, it's okay. I've been working diligently all morning so I'm due for a break."

Daniel did as Ashley suggested and pulled up a chair from a neighboring desk. He turned on his small tablet and pulled up the homes he had saved on the device. Ashley was somewhat curious and inched closer to his chair.

"Terri and I have narrowed down our final list to three homes," he said moving the device closer to her. "Here's the first one."

"Whoa, that's a beautiful home, Daniel," she said with enthusiasm.

"It's over two thousand square feet and has a big back yard," he said with excitement. "Go ahead and scroll through the pictures."

"I would definitely put this one on my short list if I were buying a home," she said moving her finger over the tablet's screen.

"Yes, but it's not our favorite."

"Which one is?"

"This one right here," he said pointing out the home on the tablet.

"Wow, now that's a gem," she said as her eyes grew wider.

"It has four bedrooms, three baths, a killer kitchen, and a garage for two cars."

"I'm so excited for you and Terri."

"Yeah, we're pretty excited ourselves. The hardest part is picking out the one we really want."

"Well, let me see the final one on your list."

"Oh, sure, it's this one here. Let me pull it up for you."

Just as he was beginning to show her the final home, Charlene walks up to the pair. She notices the two are engaged in something that seems to be interesting other than work.

"You two seem to be enjoying yourselves this morning," she said stopping at Ashley's desk.

"Oh, hi, Charlene," answered Daniel quickly. Then he smoothly placed his tablet underneath a stack of papers. "I was just helping out Ashley, with a few questions, she had on her invoices."

"Yeah, I really appreciate your help, Daniel," said Ashley lying a little.

"Don't mention it," he said standing up. "Well, I'm heading back over to my desk now. Let me know if you need any further assistance."

"Okay, I will," said Ashley smiling.

As he walked away, Charlene stood there not believing a word of what she just heard. Once he was fully out of sight, she turned her attention back to Ashley.

"Ashley, like I mentioned to you earlier this morning, I need half of the completed invoices on my desk as soon as possible."

"Charlene, I just placed them on your desk a few moments ago."

"Are you sure?"

"Yes, ma'am."

"Well, you must have placed them there when I slipped away to the breakroom for some fresh-brewed coffee."

"Probably so."

"Okay, then carry on and don't forget to give me the remaining half before noon."

"Don't worry, I promise, they will be there by then."

"Charlene turned away slowly and began to walk back to her office. Meanwhile, Ashley went back to working on the stack of invoices. Suddenly, her desk phone began to ring. She could tell by the caller's extension it was Daniel.

"Hey, Daniel," she said answering the phone quickly.

"Sorry if I got you into hot water with Charlene," he said.

"Everything is fine but I swear sometimes I feel overworked and underappreciated."

"Don't be because you're a great employee. If that

wasn't the case, the company wouldn't keep you around."

"Thanks, Daniel, I needed that."

"How about we do lunch later on?"

"Um, I don't know. I'll probably go for my usual power walk to relieve some stress."

"Ashley, one missed day without your power walk won't kill you. Plus, I'm treating."

"Okay, I'm sold. I'll buzz you in a few hours."

"Sounds good. I'll talk to you then."

The two coworkers hung up their designated phones. Ashley buried her head into the invoices on her desk. She desperately wanted to finish her work on time. But more importantly, she didn't want to break her promise to Charlene.

CHAPTER 19

Jennifer lay in the doggy-style position with her ass up and face down. He knees were on the edge of the bed's mattress. I stood behind her, with my feet slightly apart on the floor, as my hands grasped her pretty round ass. I had the perfect leverage and position to pound my cock into her wet-hot pussy. Beads of sweat were beginning to show on my forehead as we had been at it for a while. Being greedy wasn't my forte but her pussy was so good I couldn't help myself.

"Damn, Stewart, you're fucking my pussy so hard," she yelled out.

"It shouldn't be so good and I wouldn't have to fuck you this long," I said thrusting into her.

"Oh, baby, I'm almost there again."

"Don't be shy give it to me."

"Oh, shit!"

"That's right, cum on my dick again."

"Oh, shit, Stewart!!"

"Un-huh, that's what I want."

"Baby, I just came again."

"There we go, now, how many times is that?"

"Hell, Stewart, I don't know. I lost count after three."

"It doesn't matter just keep giving me that good pussy."

"I am, baby. Can't you feel my wet pussy throbbing on your good dick?"

"Yes, I do, and that's how I like it."

"You got my pussy tingling so good right now."

I kept pounding her pussy until all of her cum had been released. Then I pulled out of her as if I was done for the night but I wasn't. I could tell she was exhausted as she tried to stretch out fully on the bed.

"Oh, no you don't," I quickly said. "Keep your knees on the bed with your ass up and face down."

"Huh?" she asked sounding confused.

"You heard me. Do as I say."

"Okay, Stewart, whatever you want."

As she stayed there in the position, I dropped to my knees. I took my hands and spread her ass apart. Then dug my mouth into her soaking-wet pussy. First, I started by licking her walls then repeatedly inserting my tongue in and out of her cavity. I knew she loved that because her moans grew louder. When I felt she had enough, I moved onto her clit. There, I nibbled and licked then nibbled and licked some more. That really drove her wild. After a while, I got into a good steady routine going back and forth from her pussy walls to her clit. When I thought she had enough, I took my mouth and vacuumed all the juices off her wet pussy. Mixing her juices with my saliva, I moved to the top of her ass. Once there, I slowly released the concoction at the beginning of the crack in her ass. She moved sparingly not expecting that one from me. Before she said anything else, I began to butterfly-lick her anus. While this was going on, I took two of my fingers, from one hand, and massaged her clit. Then her pussy got wetter, so I started finger fucking her.

"Do you like it when I lick your asshole?" I asked coming up for air.

"You're so damn nasty, Stewart," she seductively answered. "But, yes, I love it!"

"Then keep your ass extended up so I can keep giving you what you want."

"Yes, baby."

For a while, I methodically licked her asshole rotating my tongue to her pussy walls and clit. It was no surprise she came again, for me, just like a naughty girl should. With her juices flowing more than before, I decided to change positions. I stood up and made her get into the middle of the king-size bed. Once there, I turned her on her side and positioned one of her legs open. By grabbing the ankle, I extended that same leg up to her head. I now had a clear angle entry straight into her wet pussy. I placed my pelvis in between both of her legs and all nine inches easily flowed into her. Still holding her leg upwards by the ankle, I used my other hand and began to finger her asshole. She loved it and began to scream louder.

"Now, take your finger and let me see you play with your clit," I ordered.

"Damn, Stewart, you know I'll squirt like that," she moaned back.

"That's what I want. Now, do as I say."

"Your freaky ass is going to have me cumming all night long."

She complied with my rules as her asshole, pussy,

and clit were simultaneously being satisfied. We both started howling like two wild wolves starving for food. Instead, we were being satisfied on lust and pleasure. Veins on my dick were beginning to show as I was almost there.

"I'm about to bust in you, Jennifer!" I screamed out as I stroked faster.

"Do what you want to your pussy, baby," she yelled back.

"Ahhh, here it comes!"

"Get it baby, get it!"

The first round of hot semen exploded into her. When she felt it, she quickly rose up from her position. Then she latched her warm mouth on my throbbing hard dick sucking it back and forth. Of course, the remaining cum quickly squirted down her throat.

"Yeah, baby, get all that hot cum you like so much," I said while I exhaled.

"Um hum," was the only thing she said with my dick still in her mouth.

When it was all over, I lay down next to her in the large bed. Heat from our soaking wet bodies kept us warm. Later, I reached down for the covers and placed them over us. I thought to myself, there was nothing in the world that trumps great sex. Then she and I quickly fell asleep.

CHAPTER 20

It was a rainy Saturday afternoon and Ashley found herself inside Fitness World. She decided to join the spacious gym only a few days earlier. Her decision came just in time as the inclement weather would prevent her from exercising outside.

Today was the first day she decided to stroll into the gym. Not to her surprise, the place was packed with eager people getting their daily workout in. The first piece of equipment she elected to try out was the mundane treadmill.

There had to be at least four rows of treadmills with each row containing ten units. She found an unoccupied one and jumped on it. After plugging her earbuds in, she tuned into her favorite Pandora channel to block out any noise. Then she set her treadmill to an unusual high rate of speed.

Apollo had just finished a weight lifting class and decided to walk into Ashley's area. He wore workout shorts, a sleeveless tee shirt, and cross-training shoes. Around his neck was a white towel he used to wipe sweat off his brow during a session. Immediately, he noticed Ashley was jogging at an odd rate of speed. She was struggling to keep up so he quickly walked over to her.

"Hey, where's the fire?" he asked.

"Excuse me," she replied removing her earbuds. Then she lowered the speed on the machine.

"I said where's the fire, Ashley? Seems like you're going a hundred miles an hour on this machine."

"Oh, Apollo, I guess I didn't realize how fast I was moving?"

"Yeah, I would suggest you slow down just a tad."

"Thanks for giving me that pointer. I guess I'm not use to running on a treadmill being that I normally exercise outside."

"By the looks of the steady rain outside your best bet is to be in here. At least you get to test the equipment and see what we're about."

"And I like it so far, Apollo. Actually, I'm glad I joined your gym."

"I'm glad you did too. Just remember quality over quantity when you're working out."

"What do you mean by that?"

"Basically, you don't have to run at top speed on the treadmill to have a productive workout. You just need a nice and steady pace to maximize your cardio."

"That's good to know. I guess I was trying too hard."

"It's no problem a lot of people tend to over exert themselves. Part of my job is to educate as well as train. Maybe you should consider hiring me as your personal trainer."

"I don't know, Apollo. I'm used to working out solo."

"You don't have to make a decision today just think about it for a day or two. I could train you here at the gym or even come to your home."

"Is that right?"

"Yeah, I'm very flexible especially for someone like you trying to achieve their goals."

"So if I booked you for a home session, how much time would we need?"

"A forty-five minute session should be sufficient enough."

"Are you sure, Apollo?"

"Yes, I am."

"Well, I normally like to work out for at least an hour and a half. You know so I can feel a sense of accomplishment."

"Don't worry after forty-five minutes, you'll be very pleased with my workout. Remember, like I said, quality over quantity."

"That sounds enticing since I haven't had a real workout in a while. I'll be sure to let you know when I decide."

"Now, don't wait too long because my training slots are filling up fast. I wouldn't want to put you on a waiting list."

"Don't worry, Apollo, I'll let you know real soon."

Just as their conversation went silent, another male trainer walks up to them. Ashley notices how well sculptured his body is as well. He briefly speaks to Apollo.

"Class starts in five minutes, Apollo," said the trainer.

"I'll meet you in training room B like we planned," Apollo answered.

The well-put-together trainer nodded and continued on his path. Ashley kept her eye on him as he looked just as delicious as Apollo. By now, she has completely stopped the treadmill altogether. She took a step off the treadmill and stood next to Apollo.

"I guess I'll let you get to your class."

"Why don't you come join me?"

"No, I think I'm going to try out some other equipment in here."

"Come on, Ashley, it will be fun. Plus, you may learn a thing or two."

"What kind of class is it?"

"It's self-defense."

"Self-defense, huh?"

"Yeah, you know like if a crazy guy comes out of the blue and tries to attack you. You'll be able to defend yourself from what you learned in the class."

"That's sounds interesting. I never thought about taking a class like that."

"Ashley, it's always better to be safe than sorry. Plus, Jimmy is our self-defense expert here at the gym."

"Oh really?"

"Yeah, he'll teach you proper technique about positioning and leverage, against someone, even if they are bigger and weigh more than you."

"So are you an instructor in the class too?"

"Nah, Jimmy just uses me to demonstrate as if I was a would-be attacker."

"Sounds interesting, challenging, and fun. I think I will join you in the class."

"That's good to hear. We can make our way over there now."

Apollo led the way to training room B where the class was to take place. Before they arrived, he gave her a brief mini tour of the facility. She really enjoyed what the gym had to offer and now felt more comfortable attending. But what she really enjoyed, so far, was Apollo. He struck a nerve in her but in a good way. Somehow he ignited a flame, in her, that had been blown out. She was anxious to see what would happen between them real soon.

PART III

THE GRAND EVENT

CHAPTER 21

Luke happened to be busy on a job site as usual. He and four of his crew members were renovating a client's home. Upstairs, two guys were updating a master bath with new tile, granite counter tops, and fresh paint. Downstairs, Luke and the remaining guys were putting up cherry-colored cabinets in the kitchen.

"Hold your end up just a little bit more, Mitch," said Luke to his crew member as he held a power drill. "That should do the trick for me to get these screws in."

"How's that, Luke?" asked Mitch holding his end up further.

"Perfect, now just give me a second."

"Sure, no problem."

Luke quickly drilled the screws into the base of the cabinets. Then Randle, the other crew member, held a level to ensure the cabinets were straight up against the wall. After the task was completed, all three men stood back and looked at their accomplishment. Before they could move on, Luke's cell phone rang.

"Luke's Construction Services," he said with confidence. "This is Luke speaking."

"Hello, Luke, I'm Jennifer with Whitaker Realty," she said in a soft voice. "I received your information from Stewart Sellers."

"Hi, Jennifer, I'm on a job site right now. Can I put you on hold for a minute?"

"Yes, that's no problem, Luke."

He pressed the mute button on his cell phone and decided he needed to take the call in a more private area. He didn't want his potential new client being annoyed or distracted with all the noise going on in the kitchen.

"Hey, guys, I'm going to take this call outside," he said. "You two can go ahead and finish installing the cabinets. I'll be back in a minute."

"Okay boss," said Randle. "We should be able to handle it from here."

Luke nodded, in agreement, as he knew the kitchen was almost fully complete. Then he hurried out the front door. He pressed the mute button again and placed the phone to his ear.

"Sorry, about that, Jennifer. I just had to get to an area where we could talk."

"It's no problem, at all Luke, I understand."

"So what can I do for you?"

"Well, I'm looking for a solid contractor who can expedite a job for me. After speaking with Stewart, he passed me your business card and highly recommended you."

"Yes, ma'am, I'm prompt and efficient. Plus, my work is guaranteed with great craftsmanship offered at a competitive price."

"That's exactly what I need."

"So tell me Jennifer what type of work are you in need of?"

"My client is selling his home and needs some minor modifications done in the basement."

"Okay, that doesn't seem too big of a task. What is he looking to do?"

"He wants a few vertical beams installed for cosmetic purposes. Then he also wants the entire basement soundproof and the one window dry walled over."

"Seems like he's limiting his potential buyers if he makes those modifications to the basement."

"Oh, I forgot to mention he already has a buyer. Apparently, the buyer won't close until the seller agrees to the modifications."

"So is this buyer planning on using the basement as a torture chamber or something?" he asked in a joking manner. "I never heard of anyone wanting to completely close off a basement."

"As a matter of fact, the buyer is a big-time music producer," she answered while laughing a little. "He plans on using the basement as a 24/7 recording studio and doesn't want to disturb the neighbors."

"Well, that makes sense. I assume since the holidays are upon us your client wants the task completed after the new year?"

"Actually, no, since the closing date is set for the end of December. He wants it done as soon as possible."

"That might be a problem, Jennifer. As you know, I'm working on a job now and have one waiting."

"I know you're an extremely busy man, Luke. But my client is willing to pay you an extra ten percent above your quote if the work is finished on time."

"That's a nice incentive very few people would turn down. You can count me in."

"That's great to hear. I can email you the basement's dimensions and photos as well. Plus, any other specifications for the job."

"Yeah, and as soon as I receive that from you, I'll send back my quote."

"Thanks so much for helping me out on such short notice, Luke."

"Aw, it's no problem at all. Now that we got that business out the way, I just wanted to say my fiancée and I are thrilled about meeting you at the New Year's Eve party."

"I'm looking forward to it as well. I'm quite honored Stewart invited me to such an extravagant event."

"You're going to love the Loews Hotel. The venue is really upscale especially on that night."

"Yes, I've heard all about the New Year's Eve party there."

"Alright, Jennifer, I guess we're all set. I'll just look out for your email."

"I'll be sending it over shortly."

"By the way, I'm going to reach out to Stewart and thank him for the referral."

"Let's surprise him together at the New Year's Eve party. I can even show him some before and after photos."

"Okay, my lips are sealed. I'm so busy I probably won't speak to him until then anyway."

"Once again, thank you for all your help."

"And thank you, Jennifer. I look forward to working with you."

After ending his call with Jennifer, Luke goes back inside his client's home. He really needed to pick up the pace now since he just secured another job.

CHAPTER 22

Friday had finally arrived and I had a scheduled day off. Every now and then, I did that to reward myself for all the hard work I put in for the company. Today, was the first week in December and already people and businesses were buzzing about Christmas. I, on the other hand, had my mind on the New Year's Eve party at month's end. Along with running some much-needed errands, I also planned to purchase and get fitted for my tuxedo.

As I maneuvered my S-class through the busy Atlanta traffic, I briefly thought about Jewell. It had been about a month since the diabolical event in the parking garage. After the incident, I put Solomon on notice about her crazy ass. Under no circumstances was she allowed on the premises. If she did show up, he was instructed to call the police immediately. Surprisingly, she never attempted to reach out to me on my cell or at the office. I was fine with the fact it was over between us. As far as my vehicle, my insurance paid the claim with no hassles.

By the time my car came to a stop, I had reached my destination called Mikael's Custom Suits. It was a small family-owned business located in the downtown district of Sandy Springs. Mikael's had been there for nearly fifty years and sold quality high-end wool suits at discounted prices. The business even had a line of tuxedos to choose from. I preferred to shop this establishment instead of the overcrowded malls.

"Good afternoon, Mr. Sellers," said Coleman greeting me as I walked through the door.

"Hello Coleman," I responded as I looked around.

"Is it safe to say you're in need of another suit for a business meeting with a potential client?"

"Not quite."

Coleman was a senior gentleman who looked good for his age. He had been with the company for a long time. If you told him your name once he never forgot it as his memory was superb. Dressing in a dapper manner and consistently wearing a bow tie seemed to be his trademark. He was very knowledgeable about the clothing in the store. With that in mind, I always preferred he serviced me.

"Well, sir, what seems to be the occasion you're visiting us for?"

"I'm in need of a tuxedo for a New Year's Eve party."

"I assume for a leisure night on the town?"

"Yes, that's right."

"Very well, sir. Please follow me."

He led the way as we passed a few isles of conservative to well-designer suits. The store was more congested than usual but I assumed it was due to the holiday season. Finally, we reached the rear of the store where an abundant of tuxedos were on display. It had been a while since I last purchased one. I was amazed how many different cut and styles were available.

"Here we are, sir," he said. "As you can see, we offer quite an array of tuxedos for your liking."

"Yes, it's pretty obvious," I said sounding overwhelmed. "I guess selecting one is going to be my biggest challenge."

"No worries at all, Mr. Sellers. That's what I'm here for."

"That sounds assuring, Coleman."

"Now, would you prefer a white or black jacket for your tuxedo?"

"That's a good question but I really don't know. What's the difference between the two?"

"If it's indeed a formal party you're attending then you and maybe a few other gentlemen will be wearing a white jacket."

"And as far as the black jacket?"

"Sir, the black jacket represents a more classy and elegant look. Therefore, I would almost be certain most of the male partygoers would opt for that color."

"Then it's settled, I'll go with the black jacket."

"Good selection, sir. We just need to narrow your selection down to style, cut, and design."

"Seems like that can be challenging as well."

"Oh, no, not at all. It basically boils down to personal preference and what you like to wear."

"Okay, Coleman, since you're the expert I'll listen to your lead."

Within the next thirty minutes or so, he suggested various tuxedos for me. He also educated me on them as well. I finally came across one that caught my eye. Of course, he suggested I try it on and I did.

"How does it feel on you, Mr. Sellers?" he asked adjusting the collar on my jacket.

"I actually like it," I answered looking at myself in the mirror.

"You look very nice in that jacket. I think you're making an excellent selection."

"Thank you, Coleman, but I couldn't have done it without you. I believe I'll take this one."

"As you wish, sir. Please follow me to the fitting area."

Once we arrived there, he summoned for a tailor. The tailor took my measurements making sure the jacket would fit perfectly along the arms, chest, and shoulders giving me a contoured fit. Then he measured my waist and inseam which were basic requirements for the pants. After he was done, Coleman recommended shoes, shirt, and, of course, a bow tie. I didn't refuse and paid for everything to finalize the sale.

"Once again, thanks for your diligent help, Coleman," I said taking my receipt from him.

"You're always welcome, sir," he said smiling. "As always, we will have your tuxedo fully tailored within seventy-two hours."

"Yes, I know but I'll probably pick it up closer to

140

the end of the month."

"As you wish, sir. We'll see you then."

I walked out of the store feeling confident and satisfied with the outfit I had chosen. Then I thought to myself how I was going to look like a million bucks on the night of the party.

CHAPTER 23

Just as I had imagined traffic was awful after leaving Mikael's. Lucky for me, I had been living in Atlanta for a while and knew the back route to Druid Hills. My plan worked momentarily, but as I drove closer to Buckhead I end up getting stuck in traffic anyway. The situation had to be a combination of Friday rush hour and the holiday season. So instead of complaining, I just dealt with it as my car inched along. Right before I plan to turn up the volume on the radio, Jennifer calls my cell phone.

"Hey, Jennifer," I said placing the phone to my ear. "What's up?"

"Hi, baby," she answered. "Are you enjoying your day off?"

"Yes and no. I was able to get a lot accomplished but now I'm stuck in traffic."

"I'm sorry to hear that. But, Stewart, you know around this time of the year it's unavoidable."

"I kind of figured that out already. That's why I can't get too frustrated."

"Well, where exactly are you?"

"I'm now stuck in Buckhead. I just left Mikael's in Sandy Springs."

"Been doing some holiday shopping, huh?"

"Actually, I just purchased my tuxedo for the New Year's Eve party we're going to attend together."

"I bet you're going to look very handsome in your tuxedo. I can't wait to see you in it."

"Don't worry the end of the month will be here before you know it. Speaking of which, have you been shopping for your dress yet?"

"No, but I plan to do so soon. Plus, I know the perfect boutique where to shop."

"Okay, that sounds good," I said as I continued to drive slowly in traffic. "So what time should I expect you over this evening?"

"That's kind of why I'm calling you," she said with hesitation.

"What seems to be the problem, Jennifer?"

"It's really not a problem but there is good and bad

news."

"Well, lay the good news on me first."

"The good news is I can still come over and see you."

"What's the bad news?"

"It just won't be tonight."

"Huh?"

"I'm sorry I'll have to take a rain check but it's my sister Ashley."

"Is everything okay with her?"

"Not at this moment, Stewart. She called me this afternoon sounding really depressed."

"So what did you say to her?"

"I told her I could come over tonight and bring some ice cream and a few Redbox movies. I suggested we could just spend time together like sisters are supposed to."

"Jennifer, I can't fault you for that or get mad."

"Thanks for understanding, baby."

"I mean family always comes first and it seems like she really needs you."

"Yes, you're right. Hopefully, after tonight she will feel much better."

"Hopefully so, because I definitely want to see you tomorrow."

"You can lock me in, Stewart, I'll be there."

We both said our farewell to each other and ended the call. The selfish side of me was starting to show because I really wanted to see Jennifer tonight. We had grown so close and tight lately I wanted to be with her all the time. But deep down inside, I knew she had to be there for her younger sister when she needed her the most.

After struggling in traffic for nearly an hour, I finally made it to Druid Hills. Before going home, I thought about Jennifer's idea and grabbing some Redbox movies myself.

I wheeled my car into the Walgreens on the corner of Briarcliff Road. Near the front entrance, of the store, was a Redbox machine. I parked my car near it and made my way there. I noticed there was man already at the machine making his selection. Behind him was a young and pretty woman waiting for her turn.

"So it's a movie night for you too, huh?" she asked glancing around at me.

"Yeah, I guess so," I answered. "I figured someone like you would be out on the town with their boyfriend tonight."

"I actually broke up with him last month."

"Oh, I'm sorry to hear that."

"Don't be he was a total jerk."

By now the man in front of her had retrieved his movies. He quickly departed to his car with his movies in hand. Apparently, the woman I was chatting with didn't notice.

"It seems like you're up," I said pointing to the machine.

"Oh, I sure am," she said looking in front of her.

She took a few minutes to make her selection. During this time, I fumbled with my cell phone as if I was busy. Finally, the woman had her movies and was moving on. She waved goodbye to me and extended a smile as well.

When I made it home, the first thing I did was take a long hot shower. Afterwards, I put on a pair of warm pajamas and grabbed a blanket from the linen closet. Then I popped in a movie on the Blu-Ray and got comfy on the sofa. After a while, the movie was watching me as I was sound asleep.

CHAPTER 24

It was hectic day for Ashley and she couldn't wait to get home and relax. As she and a few people on the elevator traveled downwards, her mind was elsewhere. Finally, the distinctive chime brought her back to reality. The elevator had reached the lobby and everyone funneled out as the doors flew open. She was the last one off and then quickly made a steady pace to the front doors of the building.

"So you think you're too beautiful to work out today?" asked a familiar voice an earshot away. It was Apollo, who was standing at the entrance of his gym, watching the crowd go by.

"Thanks for the compliment, Apollo," she answered pausing her stride. "But it's not that at all."

"Then what's keeping you from coming inside?"

"I've really had a long day and just want to go home and unwind."

"Ashley, this is the best place for that. You can relieve stress and burn calories all at the same time."

"Yes, I know but I'm going to pass on your gym today."

"Okay, it's no problem. Hope you enjoy the rest of your evening."

"You do the same, Apollo."

She picked up her pace again and bolted through the large entrance doors of the building. After locating her car in the parking deck, she entered it and headed home. Of course, the bottleneck traffic she encountered didn't make her feel any better.

Once home, she flung her purse on the counter and headed straight for the refrigerator. She retrieved a bottle of chilled wine from it. After locating a corkscrew, she gladly poured herself a generous glass of the clear liquid. She kicked off her heels and took a seat on the sofa. After a few more sips, Apollo crossed her mind again. Suddenly, she walked over to the counter and grabbed her purse and then took a seat on the sofa again. Once she located her cell and his business card, she dialed his number.

"This is Apollo," said the sexy voice on the other end.

"It's me, Ashley," she said back.

"I assume you're finally relaxing at home."

"Yes, I am. Are you still at the gym?"

"Yeah, I just finished a quick training session. Now I'm about to hit the shower and call it a day."

"Well, after you get out the shower maybe you should come over here."

"Are you sure about that?"

"Yes, Apollo, I think I'm finally ready for a workout."

"Now you're talking my kind of language. Depending on where you live, I can probably be over there in less than an hour."

"That's fine, I'll text you my address."

After hanging up with him, she took one more sip of wine and headed for the bathroom. She ran a hot bath and soaked for a while. Afterwards, she put on something sexy. Then she poured herself another glass of wine for her anticipated visit. With an hour, her doorbell was ringing. Barefoot and wearing nothing but laced lingerie, she headed for the front door.

"Damn, baby, you look good enough to eat!" said Apollo after she opened the door for him.

"Well, don't just stand there letting all the cold air in," she said with a smile. "Come on in."

He did just that and followed her to the sofa where they both took a seat. Then he removed his coat to get more comfortable.

"Do you want a glass of wine or something?" she asked.

"No thanks, I don't drink," he answered.

"Listen, Apollo, I invited you over here so we could really get to know each other first. Plus, you get to see what you can really have if you're interested."

"Yeah, Ashley, I'm interested alright. But I can show you better than I can tell you."

Suddenly, he pounced on top of her. Of course, he was much stronger than she was. He easily took his hands and pinned her arms back as she lay on the sofa.

"What the hell are you doing, Apollo?" she shouted out.

"I'm about to fuck the shit out of you," he exclaimed.

"Get off of me!"

"That's right try to fight because I like it rough. I knew you wanted me all along."

"No, I promise this is not how I wanted it."

"The hell you didn't! Now, shut up and stop trying to play Miss Goody Too Shoes."

"I swear if you don't get off of me I'm going to scream."

"And who the hell do you think is going to hear you?"

He continued to force himself upon her without realizing the consequences. By now, he was licking her breasts as she tried to squirm away. Through a miracle, she was able to free one arm and slap him senseless.

"Apollo, I'm serious get off of me now!" she yelled out at the top of her lungs.

"Oh, you shouldn't have done that," he announced with fire in his eyes. "I'm really going to fuck the shit out of you now."

She knew she was in deep trouble as her screams went unheard and unnoticed. Tears began to fill her eyes as he continued to try and have his way with her. Suddenly, there was loud bang on the front door.

"Ashley, are you okay in there?" asked the friendly voice from the outside.

Caught off guard, Apollo looked towards the front door. He took his large hand and placed it over her mouth. Remembering a tactic from the self-defense class, she seized the moment and kicked him in the groin.

"Dammit, you bitch!" he yelled out.

With him being weak and vulnerable, she then kicked him in the abdomen. Then he fell back onto the floor. She quickly ran for the front door and opened it."

"Ashley, what in the world is going on in here?" asked her neighbor standing there with a miniature dog at her feet.

"Oh, my God," she answered breathing heavily. "Thank goodness you came by."

"I was walking my dog when I heard a lot of commotion coming from your house. Now, what's really going on in here, Ashley?"

"He tried to," she said attempting to answer. But Apollo quickly interrupted her.

"Nothing ma'am," he said slightly in pain. By now, he had walked over to the door with his coat. "Ashley, invited me over and we were just playing around too loud. Sorry for all the noise but I was actually on my way out."

"You better get out of my house!" Ashley yelled out. "And don't you ever come back again."

Still agonizing in pain, he walked in between the two women and out the front door. Then he turned around and spoke one final time.

"Don't worry, Ashley, I won't ever come back here again," he said. "And besides, all of this was your fault anyway."

"And you can cancel my gym membership because I won't ever set foot in that place again," she said.

He looked somewhat broken then gave her a nasty look. Meanwhile, the neighbor's dog let out two barks at him. Soon he was in his car speeding away.

"Ashley, are you okay?" asked her neighbor.

"I'm a little shaken but I'm fine," she answered.

"Do you want me to call someone?"

"No, I'll be fine."

"Okay, I'll be near if you need me. Just call and I can come right over."

"Thank you so much for everything."

The two women hugged. Then her neighbor departed as the dog let out one final bark. Ashley closed and locked the front door. She took a few steps closer to the sofa where the incident had occurred. Then she fell to her knees and buried her face into her hands. She began to cry profusely.

153

CHAPTER 25

The weather was balmy and cold on this particular Saturday afternoon. Jennifer has just shown a few listings to a new client. She was confident he would eventually purchase the home.

Since she had some free time for the rest of the day, she decided to travel to Vinings. Of course, she like to surround herself with well-to-do people within this upscale pocket of Atlanta. Plus, one could fine an array of specialty shops and boutiques which cater to servicing people. Her CTS ended up in the downtown district of Vinings. This area emulated Southern charm, beauty, and value.

She walked around for a while primarily doing some

window shopping. The Christmas theme was in full bloom as everyone exhibited joyous behavior. Eventually, she ended up at Ella's Boutique. It was a grand establishment that didn't have all the bells and whistles as Nordstrom but you could find something that was one-of-a-kind, fashionable, and trendy.

"Happy holiday, ma'am," said the friendly worker as Jennifer entered the business. "Welcome to Ella's Boutique."

"Happy holiday to you too," she said back with a smile.

"So what Christmas attire are you looking for today?"

"Actually, I'm looking for an elegant dress to wear at a New Year's Eve party."

"Oh, well, that's even better. Please follow me and I can show you something I think you'll fall in love with."

"Okay, lead the way."

The worker did just that and showed her an ensemble she was more than satisfied with. She tried on the dress and it fit perfectly so she decided to purchase it. After the dress was wrapped in a custom black garment bag, she thanked the worker for her service and headed out the door. After only taking a few steps, she noticed a familiar face walking towards her. It was Keith and one of his many girlfriends holding hands.

"Well, well, well just the person I needed to see," she said loudly stopping the pair in their tracks.

"As big as Atlanta is, I can't believe I ran into you," he said with sarcasm.

"Keith, who is this woman?" asked his date.

"Oh, sorry, Marian," he added. "This is my former girlfriend, Jennifer.

"Don't you mean to say I was one of your many girlfriends, Keith?" asked Jennifer.

"Well, all that doesn't really matter," said Marian. She proudly held up her left hand showing off her diamond ring. "I'm his fiancée now."

"Yeah, you tell her, baby," said Keith with a persuasive smile poking out his chest. "Now, what's all this about you needing to see me?"

"I need to be reimbursed for the damages you did to my car, Keith?"

"What damages to your car?"

"Don't play stupid. I know you're the one who smashed my car window out with a brick."

"Keith, what is this woman talking about?" asked Marian interrupting the conversation.

"Baby, I have no idea what she's talking about," he

answered.

"Has there been some prior domestic issue between you two?"

"Baby, you know I don't have a violent bone in my body."

"Well, I have a receipt showing you violently caused four hundred dollars' worth of damages to my vehicle," exclaimed Jennifer.

"Marian, please go inside the boutique and pick something sexy out for our Christmas party," suggested Keith. "Besides, it's cold out here and you don't need to be in the middle of this misunderstanding. I'll be in there momentarily to pay for it."

"Okay, baby, if you say so," said Marian. "But don't be out here, too long, dealing with this nonsense."

"I won't, baby. Now remember to pick out something real sexy."

Before Marian disappeared into Ella's, she slowly looked Jennifer up and down. Then she rolled her eyes. Jennifer wasn't too impressed and gave her a nasty smirk. Eventually, Marian entered the boutique.

"I see you're still in the business of picking up strays."

"Hey, that's a low blow, Jennifer."

"Anyone, with some sort of class, would know that's

not a real diamond."

"Will you stop talking so loud before she hears you?"

"Keith, whatever you do with your ninety day fling is your business. I just want the money owed to me for the damages to my car."

"When was your car damaged, Jennifer?"

"The night you came over to pick up the box with your clothes in it."

"Listen, I promise I had nothing to do with damaging your car."

"Are you serious, Keith?"

"Yes, I am Jennifer. And frankly, smashing your car window out with a brick sounds like a female trait. I suggest you question your date's girlfriend."

"He wasn't seeing anyone else besides me."

"Don't be a fool, Jennifer, that's what all men say. Now, as far as I'm concerned, this conversation is over."

Before she could utter another word, he simply walked away and into the boutique. She watched him for a moment then eventually left.

Once inside her vehicle, she thought long and hard about their brief conversation. During their relationship, he was a compulsive liar. But for this episode, she knew deep down inside he was telling the truth.

CHAPTER 26

New Year's Eve had finally arrived. Jennifer and Ashley were at their mother's house for evening dinner. Although Mabel wasn't too happy, she tried to enjoy the meal as she sat at the table with her daughters.

"Lawd o' mercy, I can't believe y'all two," blurted out Mabel.

"Mom, please give it a rest," pleaded Jennifer. "We're trying to enjoy this good food you prepared for us."

"Don't be trying to change the subject, child."

"I'm not, mom, I just want to eat in peace."

"It really bothers me y'all ain't going to watch night service, at my church, with me," said Mabel looking dejected.

"C'mon, mom, I already told you last month I had plans for tonight," said Jennifer.

"Jennifer, please pass the cornbread," said Ashley not wanting to be part of the conversation.

"Sure thing, sis," said Jennifer extending the bowl of bread.

"Oh, and all you have to say is pass the cornbread, huh?" Mabel said looking at her other daughter.

"Mom, I can't help it if I had to change my plans."

"Yeah, but at the last minute, Ashley."

"I go to church with you all the time, mom. It's not going to kill me to miss one watch night service with you."

"But watch night service is once a year not every Sunday, Ashley?"

"I'm sorry, mom, but I still can't go."

"Well, I'm going to have Bishop Eddie Wrong pray extra hard for y'all tonight," said Mabel with conviction.

"Bishop Eddie Wrong!" Jennifer shouted out. "Mom, are you serious?"

Bishop Eddie Wrong and his mega church congregation, in Lithonia, had been in the news for a while now. For years, he was labeled as the most homophobic preacher in Atlanta. He adamantly rejected homosexuality and didn't mind openly discussing it whenever he could. Now, there was a scandal brewing how he manipulated the word and church by having sexual interaction with younger boys in his congregation. Being that he was married for over thirty years, and had four children, didn't fare too well with the community. Pending criminal and civil litigation didn't stop lewd photos of him and these young boys from surfacing on the internet.

"Yes, child, I sure am."

"But after the scandal and media attention I thought you stop going to his church."

"I did but Sister Coreen convinced me to return."

"That man is no more than a devil in disguise. He ought to be ashamed for calling himself a man of God."

"Jennifer, you better watch your mouth. You're on the verge of blasphemy."

"Mom, he's nothing more than a false prophet."

"Alright, stop it!" Mabel said slamming her palm on the table. "If I want to go to Bishop Eddie Wrong's church tonight that's my choice. I'm still your mother and you better show me some respect."

"Yes, ma'am" added Jennifer lowering her voice a tad.

While Mabel and her oldest daughter were having what seemed to be a minor disagreement, Ashley felt this was a good time to chime in. She wanted to get a new conversation going between everyone and food was probably the best way to start.

"Well, who's up for some apple pie I bought from the bakery?" Ashely asked.

"Child, you know my diabetes ain't going to allow me to touch that," replied Mabel.

"Mom, its sugar-free just like your birthday cake," added Ashely.

"Even though it don't taste the same, I guess I'll take a slice," said Mabel.

"I'll take a piece as well," interjected Jennifer.

"Good then give me a minute to cut everyone a slice, "said Ashely getting up from the table. She was glad the subject matter was going in a different direction.

"I'll clear the dinner plates off the table while you're cutting the pie," announced Jennifer standing up.

Mabel said nothing, but waiting patiently, as her daughters handled their designated tasks. Within a short moment, everyone was seated back at the table again with pie in front of them.

"Mmm, that's pretty good, Ashley," said Mabel digging in first.

"I agree, it sure is," Jennifer said helping herself as

well.

"I'm glad you two like it."

No one said a word as all three of them finished off their pastry dessert. Apparently, the apple pie was better tasting than initially thought.

"Whew, I'm full as a tick," said Mabel pushing away her dessert plate. "I guess I'll go in the living room, for a while, and let my food settle."

"And I'll do the dishes," Ashley announced while standing up. Then she made her way to the kitchen sink.

"Do you need me to help you, sis?"

"No, I'm fine. You can keep mom company, in the living room, if you want."

"Okay, I'll do that."

Jennifer stood up and assisted her mother up from her chair. The two disappeared into the adjacent room while Ashley conquered the stockpile of dishes. When the pair reached the other room, Mabel sat down first on the couch. Then she picked up the remote hoping to find Judge Mathis. Jennifer sat down next to her. Once Mabel realized her favorite show wasn't on, she turned her attention to her daughter.

"So what time is Stewart picking you up from your house?"

"Actually, I'm going to meet him at the New Year's Eve party, mom."

"Child, don't you know a man is supposed to pick you up on a date?"

"Oh, mom, that's so old fashion."

"I guess you young folks do things so different nowadays."

"It's no big deal if I meet him there. I have a few errands to run when I leave here so I don't want to be pressed for time waiting on him."

Mother and daughter sat on the couch having a good time. Mabel brought up old stories of how men use to court the women back in her day. Jennifer got a real good kick out of that.

"Well, Jennifer, this evening is getting away from us. I guess you're finna go soon."

"Yes, mom, I better get a move on. Plus, you know I have to make a few stops before I get ready for the party."

Jennifer helped her mother up from the couch. The two stood side by side. Mabel then hugged her daughter tightly not wanting to let go.

"You take care tonight and be safe out there."

"Don't worry, I will, mom."

"I love you, baby."

"Mom, I love you too."

After mother and daughter separated from hugging, Jennifer noticed Mabel was somewhat teary-eyed. At that point, she felt guilty not being able to attend watch night service with her mother.

"I guess you got everything you brought in with you, huh?"

"Yes, I left my purse in the car but I brought my cell phone in with me. I wonder where I laid it down."

"Here it is, Jennifer," said Ashley walking into the living room. "I found it on the kitchen counter while cleaning up."

"Oh, thanks, sis."

The two siblings exchanged hugs and expressed their love for one another. After that, Jennifer vanished out the front door. Ashley then joined her mother on the couch.

"You'll be able to drop me off at Sister Coreen's house, when you leave, right?"

"Yes, mom, I can do that."

"That's good because I can just ride to the church with her."

"Is there anything else you need me to do before then?"

"See if you can find Judge Mathis on the television

set."

"Mom, I doubt it's on this late in the evening but let me see."

Ashley picked up the remote and flicked aimlessly through the channels. Mabel sat there patiently hoping she would find her favorite show. Her daughter was happy to be spending quality time with the person she loved the most.

CHAPTER 27

It was half past eight when I woke up from my nap. I laid in bed thinking how rejuvenated I felt. By ten o'clock I needed to meet Jennifer as the Loews Hotel for the grand New Year's Eve party. I sprung out of bed and yawned. Then I made it to the bathroom where I needed to shave. At the sink, I splashed some warm water on my face. This would allow my pours to quickly open up resulting in a clean-cut shave. As I lathered my face with shaving cream, I thought about how productive the year had been but I still wanted to progress even more. Maybe I would follow up with Luke's suggestion and begin the initial steps of starting my own business next year.

While shaving, another thing crossed my mind and that was Jewell. Even though I was disappointed the way it ended between us, I was still concerned a little. At this point, she never attempted to reach out to me and that was somewhat scary. Maybe she had enough of me, as I had of her, and decided to move on. If that was the case, I was happy we both could move on like adults.

"Now your face is as smooth as a newborn baby's ass," I said out loud looking in the bathroom mirror.

I had finished shaving every inch of facial hair off and was quite impressed. Then I rinsed my face off with cold water and patted it dry. Next on the agenda was a long hot steamy shower. I turned the facet on, stripped out of my boxers and tee shirt, and then jumped in.

After spending an ample amount of time in the shower, I finally got out. I dried my body off completely and wrapped the towel around my waist. Then I walked back over to the sink where I stood in front of the mirror again. I combed my hair, brushed my teeth, and sprayed on some deodorant. The final thing I did was put on some good-smelling cologne. I figured Jennifer would love it.

As I made my way back into the bedroom, I noticed my cell phone's message light was blinking. Apparently, I didn't pay any attention to it after I awoke from my nap. I grabbed my phone and realized it was a text message, from Jennifer, that read: Hey, baby, meet me at 1407 Lantern Way in Kennesaw @10pm sharp. I have a surprise 4 U B4 we bring in the new year. Don't reply or question me, because remember, it's a surprise.

"Mmm, I wonder what this surprise is all about." I asked myself out loud. "Maybe she wants to light a few firecrackers before the main ones go off at midnight."

I completely followed the instructions and didn't reply or question her. Actually, I found it kind of challenging to see what was in store for us and it was turning me on. I tossed my cell phone on the bed and continued to get ready. I unpacked my tailor-fitted tuxedo and placed it on. It fit me like a well-designed glove. After I had my shoes on, I stood in the mirror admiring myself.

"Damn, Stewart, you really look like a million bucks," I said to myself adjusting my cufflinks. Then I smiled and laughed a little.

After placing my gold watch on, I noticed it was already nine-thirty. So I quickly made my bed up, grabbed my cell phone and keys, and then headed out the front door.

CHAPTER 28

My car's GPS just alerted me that I would arrive at my destination in less than five minutes. I couldn't wait to see Jennifer because I knew she would look gorgeous. The only item that concerned me was the surprise. Dying to see what it was, I hope it wouldn't take too long. We didn't need to keep Luke and his fiancée waiting for us at the party.

Finally, I reached my destination and the drive wasn't that bad. I pulled into the driveway of the nice multi-level two-door garage home that had to be at least five thousand square feet. The number above the door indicated I was at the right place. Plus, there was a 'for sale' realty sign in the front yard with Jennifer's contact info on it.

As I exited my vehicle, I notice Jennifer's car was nowhere in sight. I figured she must have parked it in the garage to be discreet for the neighbors. The neighborhood was quiet and peaceful. It was a well-to-do community because the homes were well-crafted and spaced apart for privacy. When I reached the front door, I pressed the doorbell. There was no answer so I calmly pressed it again. Before pressing it again, I decided to just turn the doorknob and simply let myself in.

"Jennifer, are you in here?" I asked out loud as I closed the door behind me. "It's me, Stewart."

The great craftsmanship of the home extended into the interior as well. There was a light, in front of me, illuminating the empty home. As I walked past the formal living and dining room, I noticed the real hard wood floors, crown molding, and trey ceiling. When I reached the kitchen, I stopped and noticed it had an open concept. The stainless steel appliances were top-of-the line. Of course, the cabinets were handcrafted in cherry wood and granite covered the counter tops. It was definitely a nice home that the seller could get what he wanted for it.

"Hey, Jennifer, you can come out now," I said but this time more loudly. "I'm here, on time, for the surprise just like you said."

"Keep walking forward and come around the corner," a faint voice said. "I'm down here in the basement."

I did as instructed and kept walking forward and came upon a large open area. I assume this would be the family room. It was empty as well just like the rest of the home. In front of me was a slender door that was slightly opened. I grabbed the doorknob and pulled it towards me. I noticed a narrow flight of stairs leading to what seemed to be the home's basement. Slowly, I traveled down the wooden stairs as they screeched a bit with every step I took. As I moved downwards, the light upstairs was gradually fading away. It seemed as if I was walking into a black hole until I reached the bottom of the stairs. This better be one helluva surprise I thought to myself. About ten yards in front of me was another door. It was slightly ajar but I couldn't see what was in the room. I did notice the room was barely lit by what I assumed were candles. Obviously, Jennifer has some sort of romantic surprise in store for us. Without wasting any more time, I moved forward once again. When I reached the door, I opened it knowing I would see Jennifer.

"Alright, baby, here I am just as you requested," I announced walking through the doorway.

"Yes, and I can see you follow directions very well,"

said the voice in front of me. "And I must say Stewart you look very handsome, distinguished, and debonair in your stylish black tuxedo."

I was so surprised by who was standing a few feet in front of me. So surprised, I was caught off guard with my mouth literally wide open not knowing what to say next. My calm demeanor quickly turned to rage and disappointment. Apparently, my facial expression was letting the person know how I felt. Before I could say another word, a cool gassy substance was quickly sprayed into my face. I stumbled backwards shocked by what I had just absorbed. I noticed the person placing what seemed to be a handkerchief over their nose and mouth. I began to cough and really couldn't see straight. Then another round of the substance was released again on me. Within seconds, I was blinded and out in a daze.

CHAPTER 29

Meanwhile, across the city, Luke and his fiancée, Kayla, were getting ready for the New Year's Eve party. Apparently, Luke has some trouble getting his outfit together.

"Honey, have you seen my tie?" he asked scrambling around in the bedroom.

"No, Luke, I haven't," she replied from in front of the floor mirror. "Check your bag you brought over."

"I've already checked it twice and it's not in there."

"I swear, Luke, you're going to have to get organized especially if we're going to be married and living together."

"Honey, I am organized. If you would have let me get

ready at my place instead of coming over here none of this would be happening."

"Don't panic it's just a tie."

"Yeah, but I can't go to the party without it. I'll look half-crazy wearing a tuxedo without a tie."

"Let me see if I can help you find it," she said moving away from the mirror. "Maybe you dropped it in the closet."

"No, I already looked in there," he said looking under her king-size bed.

"You're right it's not in there," she said exiting the large closet. "Let me check the bathroom."

"Kayla, I've already check there too," he said sounding agitated.

"Here it is, Luke," she said holding the tie in her hand.

"Damn, where was it in the bathroom?"

"On the shower rod and don't ask me how it got there."

"Thank you, honey, you're a lifesaver."

"I know, Luke, now please finish getting ready. We're already running late for the party."

"Okay, just give me a minute to tie the knot and we should be ready to go."

He retreated to the bathroom to fit his tie while she

stood back in front of the floor mirror admiring herself. She really didn't need to do this as she looked quite sophisticated with her fashionable black dress and heels on. Her diamond earrings gave off a radiant luster that complemented her caramel-color skin tone.

"Now, you look very handsome for my soon-to-be husband," she said as he reentered the bedroom.

"You think so, huh?" he asked smiling.

"I know so."

"Thank you, honey."

He quickly put on his jacket and walked over to her. Then he gave his fiancée a kiss on her lips.

"What was that for, Luke?"

"Because I love you, Kayla."

"Baby, I love you, too."

"Well, I believe we're all set to go. I'm glad you live near midtown. Are you ready to leave now?"

"Yes, I am."

"Alright, let's do this."

He grabbed her hand and led the way from the bedroom to the home's garage. Then he stood in front of his vehicle fumbling through his pants pockets for his key. She looked at him in a funny way.

"Don't tell me we're going to take your truck to the

party, Luke?"

"There's nothing wrong with my truck, Kayla."

"But it's so big and bulky."

"Don't you start getting all bougie on me just because we're going to an upscale party at the Loews Hotel."

"I promise, Luke, I'm not."

"And besides, my Ford F150 is only a year old. Plus, I had it washed and detailed yesterday just for tonight."

"I was just going to suggest we take my car."

"Dammit, I can't find my keys," he said emptying his pockets. "I must have left them in your bedroom."

"Don't worry about it," she said handing him her keys. "Let's just take my Lexus."

"Alright, if you insist. Get in, honey, I'll drive."

Within fifteen minutes, the lovely couple had reached their destination. Once inside the ballroom, the two really began to enjoy themselves. The live band was playing upbeat old school rhythm and blues. The dance floor was packed. By now, both of them had finished off a glass of complimentary champagne.

"C'mon, baby, I want to dance," she said feeling good off the liquid she just consumed.

"Maybe we should walk around one more time and look for Stewart and his date," he suggested.

"They're two adults, I'm sure they'll be okay. We'll probably run into them later tonight anyway."

"Yeah, I'm sure your right but let me call Stewart's phone right quick."

"Okay, go ahead."

He pulled out his cell phone, from his jacket, and began to call. Meanwhile, she stood next to him shaking her ass, in a sexy way, anxious to hit the dance floor. Then the live band played louder as more people hit the dance floor.

"That's weird, Kayla, my calls are going straight to his voice mail."

"What did you say, Luke?"

"I said my calls are going straight to his voice mail. That never happens."

"Then send him a text and let's get on this dance floor."

He complied with his fiancée's request and sent the text. Then he stuffed his cell phone back into his jacket. The pair disappeared into the large crowd, on the dance floor, enjoying the party.

CHAPTER 30

Jennifer arrived at the Loews Hotel a little after ten o'clock. She pulled up to the complimentary valet in front of the entrance. A friendly young man quickly assisted her.

"Good evening, ma'am," said the valet opening her door.

"Hello," she politely said exiting her car.

"Are you here for the New Year's Eve party, ma'am?"

"Yes, I am."

The young man gave her a ticket he was holding. She simply stuffed it into the small purse she was carrying.

"Ma'am, the party is being held in the hotel's ballroom. If you walk through the entrance its straight pass the lobby."

"Okay, thank you."

She moved forward as the young man jumped into her vehicle and pulled away. Soon he was out of view. She noticed a steady stream of cars pulling up, for the next valet, as she made her way inside the hotel.

Inside the ballroom, she was very impressed. The lights were dimmed but lit enough where you could still see. There were servers dressed in white jackets offering glasses of champagne. She noticed an area where hot and fancy hors d'oeuvres were being served near one of the many full serviced bars. Mostly everyone was on the dance floor while a few people were seated, at their table, watching the crowd.

"Ma'am, would you care for a glass of chilled champagne?" asked a server approaching her with a silver tray.

"Oh, no thank you," she responded," Maybe later, closer to midnight, I'll have one."

"Very well, ma'am. Let us know if we can be of further assistance."

"Okay, I will."

The polite man walked away and approached other patrons. She continued to walk throughout the large ballroom. She pulled out her cell phone, from her purse, and attempted to make a call. But just like Luke she received the same results. Becoming a little worried, she continued to walk around for a while. As she did, an older man bumped into her while attempting to walk pass her. New Year's was less than two hours away but he was already inebriated from drinking.

"Hey, sexy momma," he blurted out with a noticeable smell of alcohol on his breath.

"Excuse me," she said attempting not to be rude.

"I said, hey sexy momma," he said but louder this time. "Damn, you fine!"

"Hey, Leon, what are you doing?" asked his buddy running up to him.

"Man, I'm just having a very intellectual conversation with this pretty young lady."

"C'mon, Leon, our table and dates are over this way," pointed out his friend.

"Well, then dammit lead the way."

"Sorry, ma'am, my friend has had a little bit too much to drink."

She simply nodded and smiled at the man's friend. He quickly grabbed Leon by his shoulder and led him away. By now, she noticed the crowd was starting to swell more and more. Even the dance floor seemed to have swallowed up the entire ballroom. Once again, she turned to her cell phone to make a call. She decided to take a few steps backwards to remove herself from the crowd. Unexpectedly, she accidentally bumped into a woman walking up behind her.

"Oh, excuse me, sweetie," Kayla said. "I'm sorry, I didn't see you."

"It's actually my fault," said Jennifer. "I should have been looking behind me."

"Well, the size of this crowd doesn't help especially since I'm trying to find my date."

"Tell me about it. That makes two of us trying to find someone."

"There you are, honey," said Luke approaching the pair. He had two glasses of champagne in his hand.

"Where did you run off to when I went to the ladies room?" asked Kayla.

"I had to get us two more glass of champagne after all that dancing," he replied handing her a glass.

"Thank you, baby, I definitely need it," she said. Then Kayla turned her attention back to Jennifer. "Well, enjoy the rest of the evening and I hope you find your date soon."

"Yeah, Stewart better show up or I'm going to be

highly upset," exclaimed Jennifer.

"Did you say, Stewart?" asked Luke with a concerned look on his face.

"Yes, he's my date I've been looking for," she replied.

"You mean Stewart Sellers is your date?" he asked.

"Um, yes he is," she said.

"Wow, this really is a small world," he said somewhat stunned. "I'm Luke and this is my fiancée, Kayla. You must be Jennifer."

"Oh, what a coincidence," she announced looking shocked. "Yes, I'm Jennifer and we were supposed to meet you two here."

Everyone exchanged handshakes and a pleasant smile in the process. Kayla began to sip on her champagne while Luke continued to talk.

"I guess Stewart decided to surprise us all by being a little late. But I think the surprise we have for him is much better."

"What surprise is that, Luke?"

"You know the home modification project we discussed."

"So you and Jennifer have spoken to each other before, Luke?" asked Kayla sounding jealous.

"No, honey, it's nothing like that," he quickly

answered. "She called me about some construction work."

"I never called you before, Luke," Jennifer quickly added.

"Okay, I've had a few glasses of champagne but I'm not drunk. Jennifer, don't you remember calling me about the home on Lantern Way in Kennesaw?"

"I'm representing a client who is trying to sell his home on Lantern Way. But once again, Luke, I never spoke to you before."

"Somebody better tell me what's really going on," blurted out Kayla.

"I swear I put a lot of hours modifying the basement according to your seller's specifications. When the work was done I got paid through a wire transfer into my bank account."

"The seller, I represent, has been in St. Maarten on vacation for over a month now. He never wanted any renovations done to the basement."

"Okay, I'm really confused now, said Luke scratching his head. "Then who was I talking to all along?"

"That's what I intend to find out right now," answered Jennifer.

"Sweetie, what do you plan on doing?" asked Kayla.

"I'm going to the home on Lantern Way for some

answers," replied Jennifer.

CHAPTER 31

Jennifer ran out the ballroom and retrieved her vehicle from the valet. She pressed on the gas pedal and headed towards Kennesaw as fast as she could. While driving in silence, she had figured out everything including who the culprit was all along. Even though the pieces of the puzzle had come together, she still couldn't believe it. Trying to figure out how to rectify the situation was the best option she could come up with for now.

When she finally reached the house on Lantern Way, she pulled up directly behind my Mercedes. After turning her engine completely off, she grabbed the steering wheel with both hands, closed her eyes, and thought real hard.

Then she popped the trunk and headed to the rear of the vehicle.

There she located a familiar small metal box and quickly opened it. She pulled out a chrome forty-five caliber gun. Then she checked the revolver to make sure it was fully loaded. Snapping the revolver back in place, she made her move.

At the front door, she let herself in and approached with caution. Being familiar with the home's layout, she quickly found the basement door and descended down the flight of narrow steps. Once she reached the second door, she noticed it was closed and locked.

"Open up this damn door, now!" she yelled out banging on it.

There was complete silence but she knew there was something going on behind the door. She nudged her shoulder against the door and tried to force her way inside but failed. Then she remembered what she watched in an old crime movie. The perpetrator kicked in the door, at the knob, to gain entry into a home. She backed up a few feet and lunged forward with her right foot. Just like in the movie, the door burst open.

"What are you doing here? You're not supposed to know about this."

"Put the knife down and let him go."

"I'm not putting the knife down for you, him, or anyone else."

"I swear I'll shoot if you don't put the knife down."

"No!"

"I'm going to shoot on the count of three if you don't drop that knife."

"Go ahead, I dare you."

"Don't make me do this! One, two, three."

Jennifer fired a single warning shot right above Ashley's head. The bullet apparently struck a water line as mist began spewing from the lowered ceiling. Startled and amazed, Ashley inadvertently dropped the large knife. Knowing she was totally defenseless, Ashley did the next best thing and rushed forward to her sister. Jennifer lowered her gun and pointed it at Ashley coming straight for her. But she was like a deer caught in the headlights knowing she didn't have the willpower to shoot Ashley.

Ashley took both of her hands and placed it on the barrel of the gun once she reached Jennifer. The gun was now pointed upwards and the women were tussling, in a circle, with each trying to gain possession. Suddenly, the gun went off with the bullet racing into the ceiling again. Both women continued to fight for control.

"Don't you dare let her get that gun out of your hands!" I yelled out cheering Jennifer on. "Otherwise, we'll all be doomed."

"I can't seem to wrestle it away from her, Stewart," screamed Jennifer as if she was losing her positioning.

"Give me this damn gun, Jennifer," Ashley shouted.

"Get better leverage on her, Jennifer!" I yelled out again feeling helpless as I was tied up.

My suggestion sparked an extra kick into Jennifer. Somehow she managed to position herself behind Ashley. With their hands still raised above their heads, Jennifer was able to fold Ashley arms down into her abdomen. While doing this, both women were still trying to secure the gun. Without any further notice, the gun went off for the final time. The bullet went through Ashley's stomach traveling through her left lung, and exiting her side. She fell to the floor and landed on her back as the gun fell near her.

"Oh my God!" Jennifer screamed frantically with her hands on her head. "What just happened?"

"Jennifer, get over here and cut me loose," I loudly ordered.

She was in shock not knowing what to do next. She looked at me and then her blood-soaked sister. I yelled out, at her again, and finally she cut my bounded arms and legs loose from the beam. I rushed over to my clothes nearby and put on my pants and then grabbed my jacket. I turned my cell phone back on and dialed 9-1-1. Meanwhile, Jennifer rushed over to her sister and kneeled down next to her. She grabbed her hand for comfort and reassurance. By now, Ashley was spitting up blood attempting to talk.

"I guess you finally figured it all out and beat me at my own game, sister," Ashley said softly. "Mom, always bragged how you were smarter and more beautiful than me."

"Ashley, it never was a competition between us," Jennifer said as she began to cry profusely. "And why would mom ever say something like that?"

"You don't even know half of the story, Jennifer," said Ashley as her eyelids closed.

"Hang on little sis, the ambulance will be here any minute now," pleaded Jennifer with compassion. Tears were continuing to roll down her face. "No matter what you might think, I love you and always have."

By now, I had ended my call with the 9-1-1 operator. I took a quick inventory of the scene around us. Jennifer was still crying as Ashley was slowly slipping away. I kneeled down, next to Jennifer, and put my arm around her hoping she could find some solace.

Then we heard a set of footsteps running down the narrow basement steps and through the door. It was Luke and Kayla stopping in their tracks. Neither one of them knew what to say as they were shocked at the scene in front of them.

Suddenly, loud firecrackers were going off rapidly outside. We all knew it was officially midnight. Just as we planned, we all were together bringing in the new year. But at that moment, it was bittersweet as by now Ashley had expired.

CHAPTER 32

Early Sunday morning church services had concluded for the day. Mabel was wearing one of her favorite dresses along with a fancy hat on her head. Jennifer had on a conservative wool grey skirt and jacket which kept her warm on this cold day. Together they both stood in the cemetery looking at an elaborate marker in front of them. Neither of the two had anything to say until the silence was finally broken.

"Here lies Ashley Jewell Whitaker," said Mabel out loud reading the words on the tombstone. "May she rest in peace."

"Amen," said Jennifer. Then she placed her left arm

around her mother giving comfort.

"Lawd o' mercy, I can't believe it's been three weeks since my baby girl passed away," said Mabel as a few tears streaked down her face. "A mother ain't supposed to bury her child."

"I know, mom, but I'm still here for you," Jennifer said hugging her mother tightly.

"Jennifer, how could you?" Mabel asked removing herself from her daughter's grasp.

"I don't know what you're talking about, mom," answered Jennifer looking confused.

"How in the world did you get caught up, being involved, with your sister's man?"

"Mom, I told you I honestly didn't know about them."

"I tell you, child, these men out here ain't worth a damn! That's why I left your father right after Ashely was born."

"Mom, please lets not revisit those troubling moments right now."

"Well, I'm just speaking the truth, Jennifer."

"Can I ask you a serious question that you'll answer truthfully, mom?"

"Go ahead, Jennifer, I always tell you the truth."

"Did you love me more than Ashley while we were

growing up?" Jennifer asked looking into her mother's eyes.

"Child, ain't no sucha thang," replied Mabel looking down at the tombstone. "Why would you ask me a question like that anyway?"

"Because Ashley told me that, in so many words, while she was dying," answered Jennifer becoming teary-eyed.

"Listen, Jennifer, every mother may show favoritism to a child if they have more than one," said Mabel looking at her daughter. "But I loved you both the same."

"Okay, mom, but you remember when Ashley wouldn't allow you to call her Jewell anymore?"

"Yes I do. She was around seven years old and thought she was half way grown."

"Why didn't you ever like to call her Ashley from the beginning?"

"Because I wanted her to have a name similar to yours."

"That's favoritism, mom. Plus, you didn't allow her to have her own identity."

"It's Sunday morning and don't you dare start disrespecting me, child!" Mabel yelled.

"I just want some answers, mom," said Jennifer as tears rolled down her face. "I loved my sister and still can't believe she's gone."

"I loved her too, baby," said Mabel wiping away her daughter's tears. "But we can't blame each other for what happened."

"I guess you're right, mom," said Jennifer.

Then mother and daughter hugged for an extended period of time. They both needed some sort of compassion at that very moment. After their embrace ended, they both looked at the tombstone in front of them. The wind began to pick up as a few rustic colored leaves blew through the pair's feet. Above them, the nimbus clouds began to move rapidly as bad weather was approaching.

"It's time like these when I turn to the word for direction," said Mabel.

"And what advice does the word give for times like these?" Jennifer asked.

"Trust in the LORD with all thine heart, and lean not unto thine own understanding. In all thy ways acknowledge him, and he shall direct thy paths."

"That's from the book of Proverbs, right?"

"Yes, baby, it is."

"I just hope everything will work out for the best."

"It will, Jennifer. God doesn't make mistakes."

There was another extended period of silence between

the two again. Suddenly, beads of rain began to fall lightly. Jennifer looked upwards towards the heavens. She really didn't care if the rain ruined her hair or soaked her clothes. This time, she broke the silence.

"Mom, I think we should leave now," said Jennifer. "It seems like the weather is getting worse."

"Yes, I think you're right," exclaimed Mabel as she felt the rain on her hat. "The last thing I need to be is sick right now."

"Here, mom, take my hand," said Jennifer extending her arm. "I'll lead us back to my car."

"Wait just one minute," said Mabel walking up to the tombstone. "I need to give Ashley a kiss."

"Okay, just watch your step," pointed out Jennifer.

Mabel followed her daughter's instructions and moved closer to the marker. She carefully avoided the grave's fill dirt which still had not settled fully. Then she leaned down and kissed the top of the tombstone.

"I love you, Ashley," said Mabel leaning back up. "I'll come to visit you again next Sunday."

Mabel then inched back over to her daughter and grabbed her hand. Jennifer began to lead the way out of the cemetery as the rain began to fall much harder. Mabel took a final glance, over her shoulder, looking at Ashley's grave.

Then she turned forward and addressed Jennifer.

"Slow down a little, child. You know my ol' bones ain't a bit of good especially in this type of weather."

"Okay, mom, I'm sorry for moving too fast."

"When we get back to my house, do you want me to cook you something?"

"No, mom, I really don't have an appetite."

"Yeah, I seemed to have lost mine, too."

"But there's one thing I won't ever lose."

"What's that Jennifer?"

"My love for you. I love you, mom."

"That's so sweet, baby. I love you, too."

The pair finally made it inside the dry car. Jennifer pulled off slowly as Mabel looked aimlessly out the passenger's side window. At this point, the rain began to fall even heavier as they made their departure out of the cemetery.

EPILOGUE

Six months had passed since the New Year's Eve incident. I was trying desperately to put everything behind me. As you might have imagined, Jennifer and I had departed ways right after Ashley's death. She couldn't believe what I put her through and blamed me for everything that occurred. Ironically, the police never pressed any formal charges against Jennifer, or anyone else, as they ruled the death as justifiable.

I thought about how Ashley should have just told Jennifer about us, from the beginning, like at the coffee bar. Better yet, maybe I should have come clean and none of this would have happened. But I guess Ashley didn't want to risk the potential of losing to her sister again. Telling Jennifer would be too easy for Ashley anyway. She welcomed the challenge of finally winning against her prized sister. To make matters worse, after I reneged on our agreement Ashley was definitely in a precarious situation.

More than three years ago, when I first met Ashley, she unexpectedly got pregnant. Even so, I still called her Jewell because her eyes sparkled like rare jewels. Of course, she wanted to have my baby but I convinced her otherwise. After much pressuring, she agreed to terminate the pregnancy. I promised her we would one day have a family, the right way, which was through marriage first. As the years went on, that plan never manifested and Ashley eventually felt short-changed.

Now, I sat all alone in the Amtrak station waiting for my departing train. I took Luke's advice and decided to start my own business but in a new city. Resigning from my job, after ten long years, was hard. Somehow, I convinced myself I was making the right move. And besides, Mr. Pittman assured me I could always come back if things didn't work out.

"All aboard!" yelled out the conductor to the remaining small crowd in the terminal.

I stood up from the bench where I had been sitting for

a while. Then I grabbed my small black leather backpack and tossed it over my right shoulder. Finally, I made my way over to the entrance on the train.

"Is this the train going to Houston?" I asked the conductor.

"Yes, sir, it is," he replied.

"Good, that's where I'm headed," I proudly said presenting my ticket to him.

"Enjoy your trip, sir," he announced securing the ticket.

I stepped onto the footstool and entered the train. While walking through the cabins, I finally found a cozy empty seat by the window. It would give me the perfect panoramic view of the passing scenery to come. So without hesitation, I secured the seat.

"Good afternoon, sir," said a pullman coming up to my seat. "Would you care for something to drink?"

"No thanks, I'm fine," I replied looking at him quickly.

"If you decide later we have soda, juices, coffee, tea, and an array of alcoholic beverages to select from."

"Okay, if I need something later I'll be sure to let you know."

"Enjoy the ride to Houston and we hope you find the trip, with us, pleasurable."

"Thank you, I'm sure I will."

As the pullman left my seat to attend to other passengers, I looked outside the large window next to me. The train was moving and picking up speed rapidly. We quickly passed through downtown Atlanta as I took one final look at the landmarks and iconic tall buildings. I was excited to put my tainted past behind me and begin a new journey in life. At that very moment, I thought about Jennifer and Ashley again. Somehow, I still couldn't get the memories of As We Lay out of my head.

-The End

ABOUT THE AUTHOR

Frederick Germaine is a best-selling author and entrepreneur who has independently published his creative works through his publishing company identified as F. Germaine Publishing. His books have been distributed world-wide with tens of thousands of copies sold. He writes, from a male-perspective, under the love and romance genre. Thus far, his novels include: *Ladies' Man* (2011), *Eye Candy* (2012), *Lovers* (2013), *Ladies' Man 2* (2014), and *As We Lay* (2016).

Frederick Germaine's achievements include his novels *Lovers* and *Eye Candy* respectively earning a finalist position in the 'Fiction: African-American' category of the 2013 & 2012 USA Best Book Awards, sponsored by USA Book News. He was also named as a finalist for the coveted 2012 National Black Book Festival Best New Author Award.

With the intention to expand his brand and build a global conglomerate, Frederick Germaine plans to launch into other areas of business. This includes screenwriting and turning his novels into independent films accompanied by musical scores and soundtracks. Of course, he will continue to deliver hot love novels in the process.

Frederick Germaine graduated from Jacksonville State University where he earned a Bachelor's Degree in Business. He currently resides in Atlanta, Georgia.